THE CURVY GIRL'S DIARY

Kai N.

D1364949

Contact Information

If this novel has touched you, or your life in any way, shape or form please feel free to contact me. All of my information is listed below.
Email:Knedd84@gmail.com

Facebook- Kai Nedd

<u>Creative Team</u>
Editor- Simone Hunter-Hobson
Photographer- Mister Paparazzi
Makeup Artist- Katrina
Graphic Designer- Ashley Shepard
"To the young talented people who saw my vision and helped to execute it I am extremely thankful. Thank you so much for helping my creativity come alive."- Kai

Acknowledgements

4

Words cannot express my gratitude or my gratefulness. I first would like to thank God for renewing and refreshing my way of thinking, for gifting me the ability to create, connect and inspire others with my words and my stories. Lord, I thank you. To my mother Elaine Lovett thank you so much for not only believing in me but for helping to make my dreams come true. Your words of wisdom, support, amazing advice and encouragement is something that I cherish constantly, mommy I love you. To my Father William Nedd and Steppie Ronald Rawson thank you for constantly believing in me and encouraging me because without that and your unconditional love I wouldn't be in this place in my life. To my Grandma aka "Best-friend!" Thank you for your words of wisdom, your life lessons and the prayers you pray for me constantly, I love you. To my cousin Allison Scott, thank you for always being supportive and encouraging, I can't begin to thank you enough. And to my beautiful supporters I really want to say a special thank you. Thank you for the constant emails, direct messages and personal testimony's you beauties send me daily. Every time my fingertips tap each key on my laptop I envision each one of you beautiful, confident women. You're my canvas's, my inspiration and my sisters. I hope each of you enjoy the journey of these new characters and with every turn of the page you fall in love with their voyage of love.

Prelude

"It's still hard for me to believe that I'm letting complete strangers in on my life. I'm laying it all on the table. My mistakes, my insecurities, my strengths, weaknesses, friendships and relationships. Along with the stories of my Sister's. The pages of my lives bare all, and for once I'm sharing everything. Unfiltered and uncut."

-Kara L.

One Night Only

"S-shit." Kara hissed as she stumbled over the glass coffee table in the middle of Detrick's condo. With her heels and clutch in one hand and her cellphone in another Kara's main concern was leaving this apartment without waking the 6-foot 7 caramel covered God that scratched her itch the night before. She didn't plan on giving her expensive lace panties up; but last night he seemed to have scratched the tingly sensation that ran through her plush body. No, this wasn't a usual thing for Kara; you know, sleeping with random athletes after sharing a few drinks at a posh bar in SoHo, but she just couldn't resist Detrick's charm. He just did something to her. She didn't know whether it was his beautiful caramel complexion, hazel colored eyes, his height, his personality or the fact that he was completely tattooed. Whatever it was, it was strong enough to have her out of her clothes and in his bed.

"I can't believe I'm doing this." She whispered to herself while walking closer towards his front door. Out of 24 years of living Kara never engaged in a one-night stand, not even in college. She was always too prim and proper to do so. In her eyes and in the eyes of others she always had everything under control, but this situation was different. Instead of having everything so figured out and in full control of what was going on she allowed herself to not think for once and that resulted in her carefully finagling out of a multi-million-dollar condominium belonging to the NBA player who pleased her the night before. With her hand half-way on the door knob the raspy, low tone of Detrick's voice startled her.

"Doing what?" Detrick spoke while standing in the doorway of his bedroom clothed in nothing but his underwear. A few minutes prior, after waking up he looked over to see where the beautiful chocolate woman that he came home with was, so he could possibly get another taste of her, but to his surprise she was nowhere to be found. However, he could hear her voice echoing throughout his apartment, so he left his room to see what exactly she was doing and to his surprise he caught her leaving. With his chiseled chest on full display Kara couldn't help but to swallow the saliva that crept inside the crevices of her mouth, Detrick was delectable enough to make her mouth water. She was so caught up in staring at Detrick that she clumsily dropped one of her designer heels causing her to look up at him slightly embarrassed. Clearing her throat to speak, she tried to quickly come up with an excuse.

"Oh, nothing. Just, getting um- "Kara said while tripping over her words slightly.

"Getting ready to dip?" Detrick asked while walking down the spiral stairs that lead to his living room. Puzzled wasn't the word. In Detrick's mind he just had one of the best nights of his life and the person he had it with was tip- toeing out of his crib. He couldn't believe it, someone was pulling a him on him.

"Yeah, um. I have a meeting in a few and I didn't want to wake you." Smirking lightly and shaking his head at Kara's obvious lie he couldn't help but to get distracted by her beautiful physique. The first part of her body that his hazel colored eyes fell on were her full breasts; the same ones that peeked through the tight red dress she wore the night before catching his attention. Then his eyes fell to her thick waist and the way it curved effortlessly; Kara was bad to say the least. She was thicker than the usual females he dealt with and she managed to have better conversational skills; I mean for the brief time they spoke. In Detrick's eyes she was the prettiest female he ever encountered and in his line of work he came across beautiful women constantly. Walking towards her and wrapping his arms around her thick frame he pulled her close to him.

—
9

"You were leaving a nigga'?" Shuttering under his touch, Kara started to speak.

"Not leaving necessarily just finding my way to the door." She said causing them to laugh lightly trying so desperately to break the awkward tension that developed between the two.

"You know after last night, I didn't think you would want to leave me so quickly." Detrick said while kissing Kara's neck and caressing her waist. *"Why am I leaving?"* Kara thought to herself while Detrick's soft lips attacked her neck. I mean this fine piece of man was in front of her ready to devour her once again and she'd rather go home and be alone? What was wrong with her? Was it her pride? Better yet, fear of judgement? The last thing she wanted or needed was Detrick bragging to his friends about who he smashed the night before and how easy it was. Kara didn't want to be locker room conversation, hell she didn't want to be a part of Detrick's conversation after this rendezvous period her name held too much weight for anyone to begin to think that she was living her life promiscuously. So, she figured if she tip- toed through his condo and through the door early in the morning he'd totally forget about last night's escapade. Wishful thinking. In fact, Detrick woke up thinking about last night more than Kara did. He just couldn't wrap his mind around how beautiful Kara was.

"I really, really have to go." Kara said while removing Detrick's arms from around her waist. Taken aback Detrick tried to wrap his mind around the situation that presented itself. Any other female would've been dying to be in his presence but not Kara, and that spoke volumes about her character. She wasn't just any other woman and that was crystal clear to Detrick.

"Wait. So just like that you're leaving?" Detrick asked while watching Kara move closer and closer towards his door.

"I'm really sorry. Last night was nice, I mean it was great. It was really enjoyable I really just have to go." Kara said while stumbling over her words and walking out the door.

"Wait, so how can I reach you?" Detrick yelled while watching her full hips switch towards the staircase in his buildings hallway.

"I'll call you!" Kara yelled while opening the staircases door.

"You don't even have my-" Hearing the door slam, Detrick resumed inside.

"My number." He mumbled to himself while shaking his head and locking the door. With Detrick's mind on Kara he had to devise a plan to be with her again; if that was the last thing he did.

***

Revving up the engine in her Porsche Panamera Kara dialed her best friends Melanie and Kisha and let their voices fill her car.

"So nice to speak to you again, what's her name again Kisha?" Melanie taunted playfully.

"I believe it's back stabbing slut who ignored our calls and plans last night." Kisha answered sarcastically.

"I'm sorry girls something came up." Kara said while pulling out of her garage. After this morning's endeavor Kara had no choice but to race home to shower just to get to her office in time.

"Yeah, yeah." Kisha said through a breath. Kara could practically see Kisha's eyeroll.

"You owe us, we're never supposed to miss binge watching Insecure and sipping on Pinot Noir while rambling about how men aren't shit. You broke a vow." Kisha said dramatically.

"And you can't forget about the overpriced pizza's that we order because of Kara's expensive ass zip code." Melanie added. Laughing lightly Kara couldn't help but to shake her head at her girls.

"I promise I'll make it up to you guys, I promise." Kara said while focusing on the road.

For close to twenty-five years Melanie and Kisha have been Kara's best friends, her ride or dies, the coconut oil to melanin and the sew in to a weave. If they wanted to write a book on Kara's life they most definitely could have. Even back to the day when they were little girls stuffing their training bras, the powerful trio has always been connected at the hip. There wasn't one without the other. Not much has changed, even with them being successful career women in their own right. You have Kara the corporate lawyer turned entrepreneur, Kisha a successful accountant and Melanie a successful Artist and owner of several studios spaced out around New York. These women sprinkled black girl magic everywhere they went, their bond just added to their shimmer. Between trying to focus on the road, listening to her friends and trying to shake the thought of what happened last night, Kara was all over the place.

"Well what held you up?" Melanie asked. Sighing, Kara made a smooth right turn and prepared a quick lie to tell her girls.

"Let me guess, you had to check emails, the same emails you could've had your assistant go through." Kisha interrupted sarcastically before cutting Kara off before she could answer.

"No, I just got side tracked." Kara said while gnawing at her bottom lip and focusing on the road. She didn't want to mention her lusty affair to the girls just yet, so she kept the details to a minimal. Unfortunately, the girls could see right through her.

"Side tracked with what?" Melanie asked curiously.

"Nothing; just some paperwork." Kara said while lying through her teeth. Kisha and Melanie knew Kara like the back of their hand, so they knew something was up.

"Wait Kara, did you?" Melanie led on before pausing.

"Get some dick?! Kara, you got some!" Kisha yelled while finishing up Melanie's sentence.

"Of course not, I- I." Kara said while stumbling over her words.

"You got some peen- peen! It's okay girl you don't have to lie! It's been a year since you've gotten your back blown out you deserve it!" Kisha yelled obnoxiously.

"Come on Kisha it's 10 in the morning; have some decency." Melanie said trying to hold back her laughter.

"Thank you, Melanie, thank you." Kara agreed.

"No problem at all, you know I have your back. Now, spill the deets, I need to know."

"Melanie! I thought your ass was the sane one." Kara screamed out.

"I'm sane just celibate and I need to hear about the excitement in someone else's sex life since mine is non-existent."

"Wait, what? I tell you about mine all the time." Kisha whined.

"I know and I'm tired of hearing it and quite frankly; Bitch your ass is too freaky."

"Oop." Kara said while making a turn into the city. In a matter of 20 minutes she was right where she needed to be. At her bread and butter, the place that pays, the place she goes to secure all the bags her office building.

"Well damn, I'll keep my business to myself next time." Kisha scoffed at Melanie.

"Please and thank you. Now back to Kara, who had the pleasure of pleasuring you?"

"You know what, I'm going to call y'all back when I'm done parking. Love y'all goodbye." She said while ending her call and focusing on parallel parking correctly. She was already paying a fortune for the Mercedes she slightly damaged by hitting a fire hydrant so needless to say she needed her Porsche to be untouched and trying to focus with her crazy friends rambling on explicitly in the background wasn't going to help her.

13

Grabbing her purse from the passenger side and locking her car up she walked inside of her office building and towards the elevator. With her shoulders back and her head hung high Kara held onto her vintage Chanel purse and pressed for the second floor. 3 years prior Kara started *Figured Trends'* a Plus Size magazine that dueled as a modeling agency. She noticed how left in the dark full-figured women were and decided to create and innovate a brand that catered to thrusting plush women into mainstream media. She often remembers how scared she was to purchase this 4-floor office building in Midtown Manhattan, but she knew that if she wanted to grow her career and her brand she had no choice but to get it done. She pieced together her income from her prior job in corporate America, received a loan from her parents and invested everything into this building and her brand. She never imagined surviving 3 months let alone 3 years, so you can understand how blessed she felt to be such a success. With each floor occupied with various aspects of her brand, Kara felt extreme gratitude each time she stepped foot into her blessing.

Walking off the elevator she pushed open the acrylic doors to her personal wing of the building and sashayed to her Assistants desk.

"Great morning! Your latte is on your desk along with your agenda for today. Also, someone by the name of Kanata called, she wants to interview you for Forbes magazine. The 30 under 30 list." Briana, her assistant rambled; trying to catch Kara's undivided attention.

"Thank you, Briana. Briana what time did you get here?" Kara questioned looking down at her Rolex. It was 10:30 in the morning and Briana was a burst of energy; which meant she was probably here first thing this morning and knowing Briana that's 6 am. Kara appreciated her dedication that's partially why she was hired; so, her cheerful attitude so early in the morning was something Kara appreciated and got used too quickly.

"I got here at 7 this morning, I was running a little behind because the subway wasn't the best. I'm sorry." She said while pushing her glasses back with her index finger.

"Briana, you're fine. I explained to you that you don't have to come this early on Thursdays, these are our late days." Kara said while sweeping a few strands of hair behind her ear.

"Oh, I know. I just want to be prepared." Briana said while pulling herself closer to her desk. Shaking her head Kara smiled and walked on to her office. Breathing out a breath and opening her blinds she took in God's smile, that's what she called sunshine. Although she was feeling a tad bit guilty about last night's smash and dash her mind couldn't shift from the positives of last night. She began to have flashbacks; mostly of Detrick's sensual touch, his beautiful body, his passionate kisses and strokes. She was starting to think about it all causing her hot spot to run with nectar. Clenching her thighs and walking towards her chair she tried to shake her impure thoughts. See, although what she did was totally out of character she still wanted to engage again; and again, even if it wasn't possible. She thought back to how she fled from his home not leaving behind a business card, number or anything. And the way she left probably had Detrick happy she was out of his hair, or in this case waves. Rolling her eyes and going through her paperwork Kara tried to shake the thought of vitamin D, and the self-sabotage she committed. *She had to face her truths.*

Find Her

Clenching his steering wheel tightly, Detrick drove his Bentley through the crowded streets of New York. He spent most of his morning working out with his team and now he dedicated the second half of his day to finding "K". He didn't remember her name, nor could he remember her occupation; all he could remember was that her name started with a K. Pulling up to the bar where he and her first met he waited outside. He figured she lived or worked in the area, so he was willing to stay there until miraculously she popped up. Yes, the idea was absurd, but it was worth the try. Leaning back in his seat his mind started to travel to the night he shared with this mystery woman. Much like Kara he was beginning to have flashbacks of the passion they exchanged. He thought back to how her thick thighs wrapped around his waist, while he filled her with his girth. Her sweet moans echoed in his head causing him to yearn for her flesh. Feeling himself stiffen up he opened his eyes and turned his attention to his sweatpants. Shaking his head, he couldn't believe how his body was reacting. He hadn't had a reaction to a female like this in a minute. When you're in his position females come a dime of dozen but it's rare to find someone interesting even after you get intimate with them. K though, K was different. K made Detrick yearn for her and her mystique added to her sex appeal. Detrick needed to find her, *ASAP.*

Old Flames, Rekindled?

The wind whistled against the windows in Melanie's park slope brownstone while she stood in front of the full-length mirror in her bedroom. Smoothing her hands across the red ankle length body hugging garment, she decided to wear; she wondered if it was too much for a first date, in fact she contemplated changing into something a tad bit more conservative. In just a few hours she would be sitting across from Brenden, a blast from her childhood past. They stumbled across each-others social media accounts and were able to chop it up a bit. He lived in Los Angeles, but he was coming to the city for business and he brought up dinner and Melanie didn't oblige. Video calling Kisha from her laptop she propped it up on her dresser and waited for her to answer. Hearing that the excess ringing stopped she stepped back from the camera so Kisha could get a good look of her outfit.

"Damn Sis, where are you going?" Kisha asked. Laughing slightly Melanie parted her lips to speak.

"On a date, is this too much?" She asked while running her hands across her size sixteen hips.

"A date! With who?" Kisha screamed.

"You remember Brenden?"

"Brenden from high school? That Brenden? How could I forget his ass? What about him?" Kisha asked while sipping from her wine glass.

"That's who I'm going on the date with." Melanie said while shaking her head.

"Wait, what? How did you guys get in contact?"

"Social media."

"The DM is the devil reincarnated." Kisha said while sipping from her glass once again and shaking her head.

"Wow, negative Nancy why don't you like Brenden?" Melanie asked wanting to know if Kisha knew something she didn't. Melanie had no room for secrets and by the tone of Kisha's voice she felt Brenden had some skeletons in his closet.

"I don't know, I just picture Brenden, the dummy from high-school." Kisha said causing Melanie to shake her head. Sitting on the side of her bed she adjusted the straps on her designer heels while listening to Kisha's tipsy rant. Grabbing some shea butter from her nightstand she lathered her legs up, allowing the sweet melanin medicine to absorb into her skin. By this time Melanie had completely tuned Kisha out and refocused her attention to the positives of tonight, the last thing she wanted to do was to walk into something completely new with perceptions and judgement in her mind. Standing up and grabbing her clutch off her bed she turned her attention back to Kisha who rambled away.

"All I'm saying is, if you wear panties make sure they're edible you know just to- "

"Kisha, please keep your comments and erotica to yourself. I'm getting ready to leave out and I'll call you tonight, goodbye." Ending the video chat and laughing to herself lightly Mel grabbed her essentials and walked out. As her heels clicked against the concrete stairs in front of her brownstone she couldn't help but to notice a Black Escalade pulling up in front of her. Thinking it was for the senator that lived a few brownstones down from her she continued her trek to hail a cab.

"Excuse me, Ms. Stewart!" She could hear from behind her. Turning her head to see who was calling out her government she noticed the well-dressed driver of the black SUV flagging her down.

"Yes, how may I help you?" Melanie asked while holding her clutch close to her just in case she had to utilize her bedazzled pepper spray.

"Yes, I was sent here by Mr. Brenden Moore to take you to your reservations at *Bao,* for 7 pm." Tilting her head to the side, she couldn't believe what she was hearing or seeing. To some this may be a small gesture but to Melanie this was beyond her thoughts. She was used to dating men who weren't even courteous enough to pull out her chair or open her door, hell sometimes their asses weren't courteous enough to pick up the bill. So, most of the times receiving a metro- card or train ride would make her happy. Sliding into the luxurious vehicle and thanking the driver she looked out the window and steadied her nerves. Sitting back and allowing the cool jazz to soothe her mental, she silently thanked the man above for allowing her to open Brenden's *DM.*

***

Walking up to the restaurant Melanie stopped just before opening the front door. She inhaled and exhaled, adjusted her dress, checked her breath and proceeded to walk inside. So, caught up in the restaurants décor, Melanie failed to hear the hostess speak to her. Turning her head in the woman's direction she caught a clear glimpse of Brenden. *"Damn."* She thought to herself. Brenden looked just as good as he did in high school. His beautiful chocolate skin still had that perfect gleam to it, his lips were perfectly plump, and his styling was still impeccable. Not much changed about him, the only thing that shifted was his physique. He bulked up a bit since Mel last saw him his Instagram did him no justice. Occupied with his phone Brenden failed to notice Melanie. He was a tad bit stressed mainly about the number of deadlines he had to meet. Unfortunately, this would be the only day he had to relax while in the city, this was a business trip, but he cleared his schedule to meet with Melanie. A lot changed since they last knew each other, and he was genuinely interested in hearing where life led her.

"Hi stranger." Melanie said causing Brenden's head to shoot upward.

"Damn." Was all   he could manage to get out. Melanie's beautiful chocolate skin and thick frame caught him completely off guard. Her pictures did her no justice.

—

"You look amazing, I'm glad you made it." Brenden said while pulling Mel in for a hug. Practically falling into his arms Melanie took in his tantalizing scent. A sweet smell of Kush and Tom Ford cologne filled Melanie's nostrils while Brenden's hands gently roamed her full figure. Finally pulling away from each other they each took a seat.

"You have great taste, Bao is one of my favorite restaurants." Melanie spoke first breaking the ice. The last thing she wanted was to make things awkward.

"I figured a classy woman such as yourself would like fine dining, I had to give you that."

Gulping lightly Melanie reached for a glass of water and guzzled down her emotions. Although Brenden was quite the Casanova over text she didn't know what to expect in person. However, thankfully Brenden's words slid from his tongue smoothly.

"I've never seen Bao this empty, I'm actually shocked." Melanie said while looking around at the empty spaces around them.

"That's because I rented it out, I wanted this night to be special."

"Wow you're pulling out all the stops. First the car, now this what makes me so deserving?" Melanie asked while smiling lightly.

"What you mean? This is light mama." Brenden answered breaking down every syllable in mama letting the native Harlem in him make its debut. He briefly took a sip from his glass and then focused his attention back on Melanie.

"Light huh? Well excuse me." Melanie said while placing her hands in her lap.

"Yeah light. Someone as beautiful as yourself should be wined and dined every night." Brenden said while licking his lips slightly and sitting back in his chair; allowing Melanie to get a glimpse of the jewelry that hung from his neck. It was more than obvious to Melanie that Brenden's career as a Producer had him on a road to riches and she couldn't lie and pretend like that wasn't attractive to her. See, Mel's reasoning for being single was based off her frustration with men her age simply not having their shit together. She was tired of spoon feeding men, dealing with men who didn't have a pot to piss in or a window to throw it out. Melanie wasn't judgmental but as she began to get older her preference turned to pickiness and there was nothing wrong with that. She just wanted a man with enjoyable conversation, a career and a saving's account, that's all. And from the looks of it Brenden covers all those areas. Focusing her attention back on Brenden she took in his features. This man was well beyond gorgeous. It was something about a chocolate brother that turned Melanie on, but Brenden was a different kind of chocolate. Brenden's chocolate complexion shimmered and gleamed even in the dim lighting, his lips were perfectly pink with a slight tint due to his recreational use of "herb" and his teeth, his teeth's pearly white color brought out his melanin even more, he was beautiful.

"You good?" Brenden asked Melanie watching her go into a bit of a daze.

"Yeah, I'm good, I'm fine. So, how's life?" Melanie asked slightly embarrassed that Brenden caught her gawking over him.

"I mean life is great I can't complain, stressful at times but I'm blessed." Brenden said modestly.

"Stressful? You're one of the hottest producers in the game right now how can life be stressful?" Melanie asked while sipping from her glass.

"That's the biggest misconception, being the best in the game isn't easy. People see the big bag and think shit gets easier when in all actuality it gets harder. I constantly have to be on my P's and Q's. But, enough about me what about you, still in corporate America?" Brenden asked Melanie shifting the conversation. Unbeknownst to anyone it was getting harder and harder for him to adjust to the lifestyle he was living. He was surrounded by fake industry people, opportunist, gold diggers and the whole nine; he was drained to say the least, but he had to push through it, too many people were counting on him. Focusing his attention on Melanie he waited for her to speak.

"I'm actually self-employed." Melanie said proudly.

"Wait, your ass is selling drugs?" Brenden asked while leaning forward causing Melanie to erupt in laughter.

"No silly, I left corporate America and started to work for myself. I decided that business suits didn't fit my figure and the stuffiness of an office didn't match my energy. So, I decided to leave and pursue my passion."

"And what's that?" Brenden asked.

"Well, after spending 4 years in such a snobby, stuffy environment I started to feel out of place like I didn't belong. I felt I was too creative for corporate. I always had a passion for art, but I never pursued it because I was afraid of how my parents would react, or if the comfortable life I imagined for myself wouldn't work so I pushed my artistry to the back burner. That was until I just couldn't take the oppression of creativity anymore. I didn't even put in my two weeks' notice, I just left. I didn't strategize a plan I decided to just wing it. Fast-forward to now I have a small exhibit in the MOMA and a few thriving investments. And aside from finances I'm genuinely happy. I wake up every day with purpose and passion." Staring intently at Melanie Brenden couldn't be more turned on by the ambitious woman sitting across from him. Yeah Melanie was fine, but her mind was sexier.

"So, you just out here living your best life?" Brenden asked while breaking his stare causing the two of them to laugh.

"You can say that." Melanie said while sipping from the Champagne flute in front of her.

"Well I admire it, I admire you." Brenden said while leaning back in his chair and sipping on his drink.

For the remainder of the night Melanie and Brenden just talked. The vibe between the two was indescribable and their chemistry could be felt miles away. For Brenden, Melanie fed a part of his soul that he was longing for and for Melanie, Brenden did the same; and for this to be a first date the sparks that ignited between the two of them felt superhuman. Even when they separated for the night and Brenden retired to his SoHo penthouse and Melanie returned to her Park Slop Brownstone their minds were still on each other. And now realization set in that potentially soulmates were met, and *old flames were rekindled.*

First Date Mishap

Tapping her acrylic nails against her phones screen, Kisha continued to double text her date Roman. They made plans to meet at *Gianni's* Italian restaurant at 8 pm sharp but it was going on 8:45 and he still hadn't shown up.

"I can't believe this shit." She muttered to herself. This was her third time being stood up and she was pass the point of discouragement. Finally putting her phone down, she took a sip from her glass and looked out the small window beside her taking in the hustle and bustle of Manhattan. Out of the trio, Kisha was the firecracker. She did what she wanted to do when she wanted to do it and she did it unapologetically. Looked at as the most confident of the group, Kisha kept moments like this to herself because the last thing she wanted was pity from the women she called her sisters. With her brain flooded with thoughts and theory's she signaled for her waiter to bring her another Martini, dry with extra olives. As the day turned to night and the sun began to set Kisha didn't move from her seat, she stayed stagnant babysitting the same Martini she ordered hours ago.

"Do you mind if I refresh that for you?" A deep sultry voice echoed from in front of her. Looking up Kisha admired the well-dressed man in her presence. Debonair wasn't the word, this man was clean and dressed to the nines. The well-tailored suit paired with Givenchy loafers had this mystery man looking casket sharp. Caught up in his attractiveness Kisha almost forgot why her ass was still sitting here.

"Excuse me?" Kisha asked spewing out more attitude than expected. Slightly taken back by Kisha's tone, Carter figured it was best for him to let her be.

24

"Apologies. I just wanted to buy you another drink, but your mind seems preoccupied, enjoy your night." He said while walking away from her. Watching his tall frame swagger back towards his table, Kara felt like a total bitch. Although she didn't know this man from a hole in the wall he was being respectful, and he didn't deserve a thrashing intended for Roman. Rolling her eyes and grabbing a twenty from her wallet she placed it on the table and slid from the leather luxury booth. Standing on her patent leather pumps she began to walk towards the man she shot down with attitude. Arriving to his table in the corner she watched how focused he was on the paperwork he had in front of him. She also watched how the gold embellishments on his cufflinks gleamed under the restaurants lighting, while his skin followed suit. Walking closer towards him and clearing her throat Kisha prepared herself to speak.

"I apologize for how I acted back there." Kisha spoke sincerely. Looking up from his paperwork Carter stared at the beautiful woman that caught his eye as soon as he walked in earlier. Although he just saw her, right now her beauty was more prominent. Before walking up to her he scoped her out a bit in fact he was so focused on Kisha he started to get behind on the work he initially came to Gianni's to do. That didn't matter though, he knew a gem when he saw one, better yet a diamond. Admittingly he was surprised at her attitude when he first approached her, but he figured she was having a rough day, so he politely walked away. He wasn't expecting her to come up to him and most importantly he wasn't expecting her to look as fine as she did. Allowing his eyes to roam her vivacious figure he was eager to, get to know this beauty more.

"No need to apologize, I shouldn't have interrupted you." Carter said while looking up studying Kisha's facial expressions.

"No, I shouldn't have spoken to you that way, I'm sorry." Kisha said while extending her hand and introducing herself.

"Kisha, huh? My name is Carter." Carter said while enveloping his hand into hers.

"Well, Carter since I lacked some manners back there can I refresh your drink?" Kisha asked.

25

"That isn't necessary, but I would appreciate if you could sit and join me." Carter said while smirking slightly. Returning the familiar smile Kisha prepared to sit.

"Wait, let me get that for you." Carter said while standing up and pulling out the chair that Kisha was about to sit in. Surprised at Carter's chivalry she sat down and thanked him. Watching Carter closely, Kisha watched as he cleared the manila folders from in front of him and stuck them in his briefcase.

"You know I've been here for a while, and the entire time I've been here I didn't see you order a thing, are you hungry?" Carter asked.

"That's so nice of you but I'm fine besides I'm too annoyed to eat." Kisha said while sinking down in her seat.

"If you don't mind me asking, what has you so stressed?" Carter asked. Pausing slightly Kisha waited to give an answer, as fine as this man was she didn't know if she wanted to share her business with him or not. Sensing her hesitation Carter started to speak.

"You don't have to answer if you don't feel comfortable, I mean I am stranger."

"No, no I don't mind sharing, I'm sure it'll be therapeutic." Kisha said while pausing slightly and looking up at Carter. For some reason although Carter and Kisha were complete strangers, Kisha felt this innate notion to be up front and open with Carter which was weird because if it was any other guy she'd be through her third lie. Ignoring her thoughts Kisha parted her lips to speak.

"Well I was initially here for a date, but the person who I was supposed to be meeting   decided to be an asshole and stand me up." Kisha spoke honestly.

"A damn shame." Carter said while shaking his head.

"See, that's the look of pity I didn't want to get." Kisha said while rolling her eyes.

"I'm not pitying you, I'm pitying the idiot who had the opportunity to be in your presence and declined to show up. See if it was me, we wouldn't even be meeting here."

"Why? What's wrong with Gianni's." Kisha asked trying her hardest not to focus on how fine the man sitting across from her was. "Nothing is wrong with it, it just isn't special and intimate enough. Truth be told I wouldn't even take you to a restaurant, I'd cook for you." Carter said honestly.

"Cook for me?" Kisha asked slightly surprised. Carter didn't seem like the cooking type whatsoever. Hell, Carter didn't seem like the type of guy that he was turning out to be.

"You sound so surprised. Trust me, I can do a little something in the kitchen." Carter answered while smirking.

"Oh really?" Kisha said through a smile.

"Yep, really. When I mention to women that I can cook that's always the first thing to leave their lips."

"Oh so, plenty of other ladies had the opportunity to taste your cooking?" Kisha flirted.

"I didn't say taste, I'm sure they would've loved too though." Carter said while smirking.

"Since, you're so sure of your cooking, I'd like to give it a taste." Kisha answered.

"Anytime you're ready too, the invitation is always open."

"An open invite for cooking to a thick girl like myself is a check you better be able to cash." Kisha joked.

"Oh, trust and believe as a real man I recognize when a real woman needs their needs met. My job is always to keep her fed and well rested." Carter said smoothly. Swallowing some saliva, Kisha couldn't help but to clench her thighs together while listening to how straightforward Carter was being. As if his chivalry didn't have her running like a lake already, his forward yet subtitle remarks created a waterfall between Kisha's knees. Gnawing at her bottom lip gently, Kisha prepared to speak but was cut off by Carter.

"You know, I'm starting to feel thankful that ole dude didn't show up. Gave me the opportunity to slide in and take his place."

27

"Took the words right out of my mouth." Kisha said while looking at Carter and smiling, the same smile that remained while they sat and enjoyed each-others company for the remainder of the night and just like that a night that started off as disappointment turned itself around and transformed into one of the best nights with the opposite sex she's had without sex being involved. She couldn't thank Roman enough for neglecting to show up because if not she wouldn't have met Carter.

Kara's Diary Entry 1

The beautiful smell of scented candles swirled around Kara's at home study, while she sat at her desk with her pen positioned between her fingers. Freshly brewed green tea sat in a mug beside her while her journal lay open in front of her. Every Saturday morning before work Kara would pen her thoughts in the small stationary given to her as a gift. In this journal she shared her thoughts, her secrets and her vulnerabilities something she couldn't do often. So just like any other Saturday, this Saturday would go the same. Stroking her pen against the fresh paper, she allowed her thoughts to whisk her away.

~~Bitch, you messed up.~~ No, that didn't sound right. I prefer to keep it even realer than that. These last couple of days have me going crazy as hell. I started the week off like I normally would have you know with a leveled head, and a conscious mind and then boom shit went left. After work on Wednesday I decided to grab a cocktail at a bar near my office, something quick and simple. Walking in it never crossed my mind that a few hours later my thick thighs would be wrapped around the muscular body of a professional basketball player but that's neither here nor there. Any who, I sat at a single table in the back watching and observing the things around me. That's when I noticed him, I can't remember his name now probably because of the 3-pomegranate martini's I downed but I CAN remember how good he looked. It should be a sin to be that fine. Dressed in all black he screamed money, he wasn't dipped in gold chains or crazy jewelry but from his swagger I knew he was a man of affluence. I watched him take a seat at the bar, order a drink and retire to his phone. I don't know what came over me, but I got my thick ass up, adjusted my dress and walked towards the bar area in hopes of grabbing his attention. Taking a seat on an empty stool a few seats down from him I ordered me another martini and waited for him to notice me. I will admit it took him sometime to acknowledge me, but he finally looked up from his phone and over at me. He asked what I was drinking as a conversation starter and I answered. We laughed and joked and had enjoyable conversation from that point forward. Next thing you know we're in a taxi on our way to his condo going at it in the backseat. It was like we couldn't keep our hands off each other. As soon as we walked inside of his place we started to undress each other. I remember this part especially because of how smoothly he removed my Bra, that shit was insane. Oh, and his body OH GOD HIS BODY! He was muscular but not overly muscular and fully tattooed. His arms, his back and the front of his body was covered in delicious ink and after seeing that I went wild, I mean he had my body reacting in a way it never reacted before. Hours later and 3 condoms later SMH. I was tip-toeing out of his place embarrassed as hell. I mean in his mind I was probably just another groupie he smashed and dashed and that's what I feared the most you know? Well at this point hopefully I'm out of sight and out of his mind at least that's what I hope for my own sanity.

-K. L

Can't Stop

"49,50." Detrick exhaled while placing one of the weights he clutched tightly down beside him. After strength and conditioning with the team, he decided to come home and do some weight lifting on his own. The first game of the season started in a week and he wanted to be sure that he was in tip-top shape. If one thing was for certain it was Detrick's seriousness towards the game. Number one draft pick, 3-time championship player and MVP recipient; Detrick cherished what basketball did for him and how it helped him provide for himself and his family. It was a true blessing and every day that passed he thanked the man above for giving him the opportunity to do so. Standing up and adjusting his shorts he walked in his bedroom, towards his bathroom and straight to the shower. In just a few hours he had a dinner date with his little sister and he wanted to be sure to make it on time. Stepping in the shower he grabbed his wash cloth, shower gel and lathered up. Closing his eyes and allowing the beads of hot water to relax the tension in his muscles his thoughts once again traveled back to "K". Detrick couldn't understand for the life of him why he couldn't stop thinking about this woman, but he needed to get to the bottom of it soon because he was starting to feel borderline obsessive. After unsuccessfully trying to shake his thoughts of her he finally gave up and gave in to them. The silhouette of her thick naked body hit him first. He could remember how beautiful her ass looked when he slid in from the back. He could also remember how tight and wet she was and how for a moment she had some control over him. Grabbing his member and stroking it slowly he dipped his head back and allowed the details from their steamy encounter to completely take over him. Her moans filled his head while his other head began to fill as well. Tugging and stroking he could feel his breaths and pace quicken. Leaning back against the wall he tried to gather his composure while his seed started to spill over. Catching his breath Detrick looked over and began to speak to himself.

"This shit is crazy." Were the only words he could mutter. Cleaning himself up again he tried his hardest to process what and why after all the other one night stands he engaged in, this was the only one doing him this way. He wondered why he couldn't stop thinking about the *Curvy Beauty that had him all caught up.*

***

Glancing down at his watch, Detrick blew out a breath while he waited for his little sister. Her ass was going to be late to her own funeral he was convinced. 15 minutes later she came into the restaurant with both arms flooded with shopping bags. Gia was to say the least spoiled and Detrick and his father were to blame. She was spoiled before Detrick got into the league, but after he was drafted she but the S, in spoiled. Detrick didn't mind it at first because he knew she deserved it. Gia stayed on honor roll, dean's list and above and wasn't a loose cannon so he figured what was a car, a credit card and some designer items. However, these last couple of months he was beginning to question if he was turning her into a monster.

"I'm so sorry I was late brother, my personal shopper at Saks called and you know I couldn't pass it up. But, I didn't come empty handed, here you go." Bria said while fishing though her bags and pulling out a Cartier money clip.

"Gia, you give me the same gifts each time you splurge. None of those credit cards better be maxed out." Detrick said while taking the clip from her hand and placing it in his pocket.

"So ungrateful." She said while shaking her head and blowing out a breath.

"Yeah, yeah whatever. What do you need from me?" Detrick said while taking a swig of his cognac and guzzling it down smoothly.

"Rude and ungrateful a two for two your ass is on a roll today."

"Gia, come on now I have things to do."

"Fine. I need you to connect me with some people in the plus size modeling world." Scrunching his face up, Detrick tried to understand what she was talking about.

"Gia do I look like an agent? I play basketball that's it."

"Come on Dee, you're well connected can't you make some calls?" She asked.

"Calls to who?" He asked.

"Ok for starters, Kara Moore." She said while grabbing her phone from her purse and showing Detrick a picture. Frozen in place, all Detrick could do was grab the studded phone case from his sister's hand and look over the picture of the mystery woman he's been searching for. Stale faced, and shocked Detrick ran his thumb against his sister's glass screen and allowed his mind to replay the moment he first spotted Kara in the bar. She did say her name was Kara, and it was almost as if everything started to come back to him. Her name, her smile, her body, just everything.

"Brother, are you okay?" Bria asked noticing her brothers sudden delay in words.

"I'm good, send me over her information and I'll see what I can do." Detrick responded while mentally concocting a plan to get Kara in his space again, *at last he found her*.

Surprise

Sitting in her office, Kara continued to fill out paperwork. Working on Saturday's while her employees were off was something that brought her peace. She was able to walk the luxury office space she purchased 3 years ago and thank God for what this office has done for her. Leaning forward and lighting a few sweet-smelling candles on her desk, she closed her eyes and began to meditate on the simple things that gave her peace. Deep into her thoughts she failed to hear the few knocks on her office door. Knocking once more, Detrick clutched a few flowers in one hand and his sister's headshots in another. Truth be told he could care less about Bria's request, he was more so focused on laying his eyes on the curvy Nubian queen that had him fantasizing about their one -night rendezvous. Before knocking once more Detrick adjusted his clothing and the **Audemars Piguet** on his wrist. He was starting to get nervous which was a rarity for him. Detrick was quite the charmer, it was almost as if suave was in his presence. He didn't have to do much the coolness in his personality alone did a number on women. So, his sweaty palms, and the slight jitters he was experiencing puzzled him.

"Man, get your shit together." He coached himself while balling his hand into a fist and knocking on the door once more. Jumping from her chair slightly, Kara looked down at her watch and then back at the door. She wasn't expecting Briana for another 3 hours and she didn't schedule any meetings today, so she wasn't sure who it was on the other side of the door.

"I'm coming!" She yelled out while sliding into her Chanel slip-on's and shuffling towards the door. Opening it up she couldn't believe who it was. It was him! The man who had her body feigning for more, the man whose been invading her thoughts for days, the same man who she left the morning after her very first one-night stand. *It was that man, thee man.*

"Hey." Detrick spoke first while stroking the bottom of his chin. In his car he rehearsed an entire monologue of all the smooth things he would say to Kara however, instead when the opportunity was finally presented to him all he could muster up was a musty "Hey". Quite honestly, Kara's appearance had his thoughts caught up. Unlike the night at *Zu Bar*, Kara was dressed simpler. Clothed in a two-piece cropped velour sweat suit, no makeup and a high ponytail Detrick was struck by Kara's natural beauty, and her natural body. Noticing how her wide hips and thick thighs spread, Detrick's mind instantly went to the gutter leaving his facial expressions on full display. Watching the tall, gorgeous man in front of her lick his lips hungrily, Kara tried to keep her composure however she too was having a staring contest of her own. Kara had to admit, Detrick was way finer than she last remembered. Underneath his simple gray sweat suit, she reminisced on his gorgeous body. His muscular arms that wrapped around her thick waist tightly, his defined ABS and v-cut and how could she forget about his…. Trying her hardest to regain her purity and stop the flood between her legs she decided to greet him casually.

"Hi." She said while staring up at Detrick intently.

"Can I come in?" Detrick asked. Nodding her head yes, Kara moved to the side and watched him swagger towards the couch in her office.

"I hope I'm disrupting you." Detrick said while looking over at the candles Kara burned.

"No, you aren't, not at all." Kara said while leaning forward and blowing out her candles, giving Detrick the perfect view of her full bottom. Cracking his neck from side to side, Detrick sat up and watched as Kara leaned on her desk and stared at him.

"You aren't going to sit by me?" Detrick asked.

"I've been sitting all morning I can stand." Kara said lying through her teeth. The real reason why she decided to stand and not sit near this Adonis of a man is mainly because she wasn't sure what she was capable of. Truth be told she wanted to pounce on Detrick at this very moment, but she learned from her mistakes the night before.

"Fine, I'll stand too." Detrick said while standing up and walking towards Kara's resting space. Face to face with their lips centimeters apart, their minty breathes entered each other's nostrils. The sexual tension was so thick a knife couldn't cut through it.

"Why'd you run out on me the other night?" Detrick asked.

"I had too." Kara answered.

"Had too? Why'd you have too?" Detrick questioned.

"To save myself from the embarrassment. I barely knew you, still barely know you and I granted you access to my most prized possession." Kara spoke honestly.

"And what's wrong with that?" Detrick asked.

"What do you mean what's wrong with that? I'm a lady." Kara fired back quickly.

"So, because we shared a night of passion, that makes you less of a lady?" Detrick challenged.

"It's hard to explain, it really is. It's just- I never really had a one-night stand before. Then my mind started to go crazy thinking about what you probably thought about me, it was just too much." Kara admitted. Shaking his head and looking back at Kara, Detrick parted his lips to speak.

"You know what I was thinking after you fled from my crib that morning?"

"What were you thinking?" Kara asked.

"How was I going to get you back there. Not just for sex, but for conversation. Truth be told these last couple of days I've been looking all over the city for you, I mean I even sat at that same bar hoping to see you again. It's crazy I know, but you intrigued me that much." Detrick said while staring at Kara. There was silence, complete silence. Their eyes however, their eyes were having a conversation of their own. Moving in closer Detrick gripped Kara's chin gently and pressed his lips against hers.

"I want to know more about you." Detrick said while pecking Kara's lips once more. Pulling back gently Kara looked in Detrick's eyes and bit her bottom lip slightly.

"I want to know what you like." He said while kissing her again.

"I want to know what you don't like." He smashed his lips into hers slowly once more.

"And I want to know what I have to do to make sure no-one else ever has the ability to do this. Detrick said while Swiftly propping her up on her desk. Making room to place Kara on the small desk properly he pushed a few things to the side and positioned her just right. Sharing sweet, sensual kisses they began to undress each other, and it was almost as if all the things Kara mentioned previously went right out the window. At that moment, Kara needed Detrick and Detrick needed Kara. Their sweet sensual kisses transformed into aggressive, eager, hungry ones. And the lust that filled the air was intoxicating.

"Take this shit off." Detrick spoke aggressively while unzipping Kara's sweat suit top and tossing it on the floor.

"Sss." Kara moaned while Detrick leaned forward and began to kiss and gently bite at her neck. Pulling at the draw string on Detrick's sweats Kara quickly gained access to what she'd been craving.

"I need it." Kara moaned while rubbing Detrick through his briefs.

38

"Take it then baby." Detrick muttered while pulling down any remnants of her clothing. Pulling Kara forward Detrick prepared to slide in with ease only to be stopped. "Wait, a condom." Kara moaned while kissing on Detrick aggressively. "It's in my wallet." Detrick groaned while matching Kara's aggressive kisses. "Please get it, please." Kara moaned louder. Breaking apart from each other for a split-second Detrick grabbed the golden wrapper from his wallet while Kara continued to get undressed. "Hurry up." Kara moaned while rubbing her nipples preparing for Detrick's girth to fill her up. Quickly putting the condom on; Detrick walked back over to Kara and positioned himself between her thick thighs. "Mmmmmm!" Kara moaned while Detrick slid into her wet mound. Tilting his head back Detrick quickly adjusted to Kara's tight wetness. He began to give her deep slow passionate strokes. Kara couldn't believe the sensation that filled her body, no other man made her feel this way and quite frankly the electricity that ran through the two was enough to make Kara think about how dynamic of a match the two of them were. "Look at me." Detrick said sternly while grabbing Kara by the neck. Looking in his eyes Kara began to tighten up around Detrick, sending him into a frenzy. Detrick was slipping and losing control, however he was determined to take of it back. He went through a lot to find Kara again and he'd be damned if he couldn't savor this moment. Pulling out he quickly laid Kara down and began to feast on her natural juices, his tongue tortured Kara's engorged love bud sending her over the edge.

Kara couldn't believe the way Detrick was making her body feel, as her eyes began to roll back in full bliss she couldn't help but to bask in Euphoria. Gnawing at her bottom lip she could feel herself on edge and Detrick could feel it too. Swiftly removing his mouth from Kara's hotspot, he filled her up once more with his girth causing Kara to go wild. With Kara wetter than ever, Detrick knew he wouldn't last very long.

"Fuuuu- shiii!" He screamed while pulling Kara closer to him, continuing to pummel her wetness.

"I'm about too!" Kara screamed while she breathed uncontrollably.

"Me too, me too." Detrick responded while trying to keep a steady pace. With their bodies meshing together simultaneously a mess was guaranteed. Kara's desk rocked harder and harder while the pair's moan and groans grew louder and louder. Releasing at the same time, Kara and Detrick struggled to catch their breathes. Kara's head rested on Detrick's chest while his head rested on top of hers. Finally, able to restore a steady breathe Detrick spoke tiredly.

"You hungry?" He asked causing them both to erupt in quiet laughter.

"Yes, I'm hungry." Kara responded with her eyes closed.

Both hungry, satisfied and confused Kara and Detrick both tried to get themselves together. They couldn't make sense of their situation they just knew whatever it was, was satisfying. Kara grabbed her clothes while Detrick did the same; all in silence. No, it wasn't awkward however it was very telling on their behalf. They were both just trying to wrap their minds around what just took place. And how they were going to move forward.

***

Holding the menu close to her; Kara tried to mentally process what was taking place. After a mid-afternoon fling of passion with Detrick they decided to grab something quick at the Diner a few doors down from Kara's office. Unbeknownst to Detrick, Kara's mind wasn't on the greasy food around her; her mind was on whether to treat this as a date or keep it as a fling. Her mind continued to roll with thoughts while Detrick sat across from her admiring her beauty. Feeling Detrick's eyes piercing into her she paused her thoughts and placed the menu down in front of her.

"Why are you looking at me like that?" Kara asked.

"What, I can't look at you?" Detrick asked.

"You can look, not stare." Kara said through a slight smile while sipping from her straw.

"Alright fine. I won't look at you then." Detrick said sarcastically while looking up at the ceiling.

"Come on, that's not what I mean." Kara said while sucking her teeth and laughing.

"I'm just respecting your wishes, that's all." Detrick said while laughing and sitting back in the booth they shared.

"Yeah, yeah." Kara said while twiddling with the wedge of lemon in her water.

"Can I ask you something though?" Kara asked.

"Ask me anything I'm an open book." Detrick said while licking his bottom lip slightly.

"How'd you find me? I mean I didn't leave a card or anything. How'd you find me?" She asked honestly. After Kara and Detrick cooled down, that question popped in her brain almost instantly and she was dying for an answer.

"This might sound crazy, but my little sister found you for me."

"Huh?" Kara asked while scrunching her face up, confused as ever.

"Not like that. See, my little sister wants to be a model and according to her you're the best in the business. So, one day at lunch randomly she asked me to get in contact with someone who could help her career I asked her who and she showed me your social media account, not even knowing that I was driving myself crazy trying to find your info. The universe has its way of gravitating two people together, so I decided to seize that moment and pop up on you. Not before stalking your gram for a couple of hours." Detrick said while resting his hands in his lap.

"So, you were trying to find me?" Kara asked truly intrigued.

"Hell, yeah and going crazy doing so. I don't know what it is, but it's something about you, that has me drawn to you. I can lie and say sex doesn't play a part in me wanting to be around you because then that wouldn't be authentic of me, but I can't say it's just sex either. While we sat at the bar that night, along with your curves I admired your conversation. You weren't forcing anything, you weren't infatuated with the fact that I played ball even after I told you that's what I did for a living and your energy wasn't fake or made up. That shit alone, had me drawn to you. You don't know how many times I sit across from females and their only focus is on what I can give them or what kind of bag I can get them. Mind you they can be complete strangers, they just think because they're attractive and I'm wealthy I owe them something. But that wasn't the case with you, you even went for your wallet to pay for our drinks, even after I had to beg you not too. That just added to the attraction I already had for you. You know?" Detrick said while sitting back.

"Well, since we're being honest, I can't help but to admit that as soon as you entered into that bar my eyes were zoomed in on you. It wasn't just because you were handsome, but it was the way you carried yourself. You weren't doing too much, and you weren't decked out in ridiculous jewelry. Your presence announced itself and that right there was more than a turn on. I didn't think you'd notice me though especially after sitting at the bar for a while waiting for you to acknowledge my presence, I was about to leave but then you struck up conversation and it was almost like I was glued to that bar stool; I was hooked from that point forward." Kara said perking up slightly.

"Trust me I noticed you, I was just waiting for the perfect time to say something." Detrick said while staring at Kara.

"I'm happy you did." Kara spoke honestly while reaching for her glass and taking a sip of water.

"Now can I ask you something?" Detrick asked.

"Sure, anything." Kara answered.

"Now I know I asked you this already, but I want to ask you again, why'd you rush out my place that morning? Better yet, why'd you rush out without leaving anything for me to get in touch with you? It's almost like you didn't want me to be around you." Gulping her water, Kara parted her lips to speak.

"Truth be told I was embarrassed. I didn't know what type of person you were at the time all I could think about was being exposed as one of the latest jump offs you smashed and dashed. So, before anything could go any further, I left." Kara said while looking at Detrick and back at the, menu in front of her. Shaking his head Detrick couldn't believe what he was hearing, and he couldn't help but to wonder what type of Men Kara was used too. Detrick was 25, and he entered the league when he was 19, he had his share of passing around names but at that point in his life, that earned him cool points, now he would just look like a fool. Looking over at Kara he parted his lips to speak.

"Kara, I'm grown. I don't discuss what I do with anyone, period." Sighing lightly and leaning forward, Detrick continued to speak.

"Listen, I really want to get to know you for you, just give me a chance too. Can I get that chance?" Detrick asked passionately while reaching out for Kara's hand. Looking down at their hands joined together and then back up at Detrick, Kara knew that although this situation was slightly odd in terms of how they found each other she knew that potentially they could be something powerful. So, she gave her answer and went with her gut instinct.

"It's worth a try." She said with a smile while running her thumb along Detrick's knuckles. And just like that, the journey of Detrick and Kara began.

Vibe with Me

Standing in front of the blank Canvas in front of her, Melanie prepared to create a masterpiece. Oil paints, and fresh brushes occupied her small studio while a glass of wine sat beside her. The sultry sounds of cool jazz echoed throughout her mind, while she tapped her foot to the rhythmic beat. This, was the life in Melanie's eyes. Wrapping herself into her art and blocking out anything non-inspirational is what fueled her fire. This setting was far from the stiffness of an office and much closer to her purpose. Beginning the silhouette of a curvy figure Melanie allowed her brush to stroke strenuous streams of creativity. Leaning back and taking a glance at the neutral colors in her painting she decided to add a pop of color. Dipping her brush into a bright red and orange fusion Mel, couldn't help but to smile at the black beauty in front of her. Briskly painting away a slight buzz from the outside of her studio took her out of her zone. Looking through the large tinted windows in her studio storefront, an infectious smile began to spread when she noticed who it was. Placing her brush down Melanie walked towards her front door to let Brenden in. She wasn't expecting him; however pop-up visits were beginning to become his thing and Melanie greatly appreciated each one of his unexpected arrivals. After their dinner date a few weeks ago, it was almost as if Brenden and Melanie were inseparable. Keeping everything extremely lowkey and under wraps; not a soul knew of their existence not even the girls. For all they knew Brenden and Melanie shared one date and that's about it; quite frankly that's how Melanie wanted to keep it, for now.

"Hey you." Melanie smiled while staring at Brenden. Even on a chill day he managed to maintain his fly. Clothed in a *Gucci* sweatshirt, *Nepenthes* track pants and *Nike Off White Presto's* Melanie couldn't stop her mouth from watering at how well put together this Chocolate man was.

"What's up beautiful, I was in the neighborhood and decided to drop by." Brenden said as chill as can be. A handful of roses occupied one hand while a black plastic bag occupied another. Truth be told Brenden wasn't in the neighborhood, in all actuality he was in Queens at a small studio deeply engrossed in his work when his mind went to Melanie, so he figured why not pop-up and surprise her?

"What are you doing in Brooklyn at this hour? I thought you were in the studio." Melanie said through a smile while wrapping her arms around Brenden and allowing him to walk in. With his hands full Brenden tried his hardest to hug her back without losing balance.

"You're asking a whole lot of questions." Brenden said with a smirk while walking behind Melanie and further into her studio. Taking in his view Brenden couldn't help but to sink his teeth into his bottom lip; he watched as Melanie switched her thick hips and full ass and couldn't help but to thank god for how fine she was. Simply dressed in a hip hugging pair of red and black plaid pants, a basic **Supreme Box Logo Tee** and **Gucci Princeton Slippers** Melanie was not only comfy but just as fly as Brenden and Brenden couldn't help but to notice it. One of the first things that attracted Brenden to Melanie was how dope she was. Even back in high school Melanie managed to be the prettiest in the room and she always managed to stand out in Brenden's eyes. It just blew Brenden's mind how things came back full circle. Ignoring his thoughts Brenden broke the small seconds of silence and spoke.

"I came baring gifts." He said while handing the fresh flowers over to Melanie first. Smelling them, Melanie leaned in and kissed Brenden's cheek sweetly. See, Melanie was a diehard romantic and she craved things like surprise visits and flowers. In her opinion it showed a side of Brenden that she was sure others couldn't see.

"Thank you so very much." She answered sweetly.

"And I figured you might be hungry, so I stopped by the store and picked us up something." He said while handing Melanie a black plastic bag.

"You brought food too? How'd I get so lucky." Melanie said while her smile continued to spread.

"This is simple mama, I just wanted to bring you something to make you smile." Brenden said while his heavy Harlem accent oozed from his soft lips smoothly.

"Open the bag though." Brenden said with a smirk. Separating the plastic handles Mel couldn't help but to laugh, smile and embrace the whiff of nostalgia in front of her.

"Brenden, a chopped cheese, a macho mango and a bag of chips? You remembered the high school classic?" Melanie blurted out while letting her mind travel back to her high school days. Back when she wore Juicy sweat suits and attended S.T.E.M High. Every day after school all the high-schoolers would crowd this one Bodega and order almost the same thing. A chopped cheese, lettuce tomatoes, ketchup and mayo on a roll with a macho mango juice on the side accompanied by any other fatty food they could find. And although that may have been diabetes in a bag it was a memory lodged in every Harlem student's mind.

"You know I had to refresh your memory." Brenden said while laughing.

"You did just that, follow me." Melanie said while walking towards the back of her studio towards her modest home away from home. She wanted to be sure that when she got this space remodeled the contractors were sure to add on a small room that paled comparison to a small condo in Manhattan so when she'd stay late she didn't have to worry about traveling home. It was proving to come in handy.

"Ooh shit, check you out." Brenden said while admiring the space around him. Melanie really provided a dope life for herself and that alone turned him on, her beauty was just a plus.

"Please, I'm just trying to get like you." Melanie said while walking towards the couch.

"Na' baby-girl you most definitely got me beat." Brenden said while plopping down on her suede sofa.

—

"I beg to differ; how was your day though?" Melanie asked while sitting beside Brenden.

"It was pretty chill worked on a few albums paid a couple of bills you know reg, shit. What about you?"

"I spent all day painting, just freeing my mind. Hence my phone being off." Melanie said while sinking back and into Brenden's arms.

"I respect it mama, you need your creative space." Brenden said while wrapping his arms around Melanie's thick frame.

"You know the other night when we were on the phone and you were telling me about how you extended your trip for a few more days I couldn't help but to get happy and sad. Happy because I could spend some more time with you and sad because I won't have direct access to you after these few days are up and it kind of sucks." Melanie said honestly.

"Don't think like that. Whenever you're missing me hop on a flight and come see the kid. Let me show you around LA."

"As tempting as that may sound I have a lot going on here in terms of new investments so hopping on a flight to anywhere is out of the question." Melanie said while tracing the tattoos on Brenden's arm gently.

"I understand just try to entertain the idea, okay?" Brenden asked while resting his hand on Melanie's thigh. Nodding her head Melanie closed her eyes and enjoyed the small moment of intimacy that Brenden and she shared.

After only 3 weeks of dating and feeling out each other's' vibes Melanie felt that her connection to Brenden was extremely strong; so strong it was hard for her to wrap her mind around it. Any outsider looking in would automatically jump to thinking the fresh young couple were dating for years that's how present and powerful their connection was. Regardless of the setting or arena their eyes always gravitated to each other and rarely left their sight. It was a vibe indeed; *a very strong vibe.*

Something "Knew"

Standing in front of Carter's apartment door, Kisha tried her hardest to get her emotions together. After ignoring a few of Carters text after their impromptu date At Gianni's she finally decided to answer him back. A few texts in, he offered to cook for her and even though she had a few reservations she went against her doubts and accepted his offer. Fast forward to now she's getting ready to indulge in a lovely homecooked meal prepared by Carter for her pleasure.

Curling her perfectly manicured hands in a ball, Kisha knocked on Carters door gently and gnawed at her bottom lip while she waited for him to answer. Blowing out a breath she prepared to knock again only to be stopped by Carter thrusting his door open. Standing before Kisha was a complete visual of the man who stood in; when she was stood up by Roman not too long ago. His muscular, tall stature combined with his handsome facial features had Kisha in a daze.

"Hello beautiful." Carter spoke smoothly. Closing her eyes gently Kisha couldn't believe how fine, Carter was. Unlike the night they first met Carter was dressed a tad bit more laid back, however still expensive to say the least. Clothed in a **Helmut Tee, Amari Biker Jeans and Balenciaga Trainers** he still was best dressed in Kisha's eyes. So, fixated on Carter's appearance, she hadn't realized that for at least a minute straight he was trying to invite her in.

"Kisha, would you like to come in?" Carter asked once more.

"Oh, I'm sorry yes I'd love too." She answered while quickly snapping out of her daze.

"No problem, come in." Carter said while moving to the side and allowing Kisha's curvaceous frame to sashay in front of him.

"It smells amazing in here." Kisha said while absorbing the zesty lemon aroma all while   observing Carters place. This was most definitely a bachelor pad however the architect and space in his Condo was everything.

"Well I prepared something I hope you enjoy." Carter said while walking further into the large apartment.

"And what's that?" Kisha asked while looking around, taking in the ambiance in front of her.

"I decided to sauté some fresh green beans in truffle oil just to get your pallet ready for the roasted rack of lamb I let marinate the night before and then to bring the entire meal together I added some rosemary roasted potatoes. Oh, and I can't forget about desert I went down to Grace's Market in the village and purchased 2 dozen chocolate strawberry's, you know? Just to balance out the savory. Just something light." Carter said with a smirk. Impressed, Kisha looked back at him and smiled.

"You weren't playing when you said you could cook." Kisha said while handing Carter a bag with a bottle of wine.

"I don't talk just to talk, whatever I let leave from my lips I make sure its truthful. There's nothing worse than a liar." Carter said while fishing through the bag Kisha handed to him. Impressed he looked at Kisha and commended her on her choice of wine.

"Okay, a bottle of Rombauer Chardonnay, a wine expert?" Carter questioned while taking the expensive bottle from Kisha.

"Yep. There's nothing better than a nice glass of wine with a savory meal."

"True enough. Let me take this to the fridge, please make yourself comfortable."

"Ok. Where's your restroom?" Kisha asked sweetly.

"Down the hall to the right." Carter said while pointing down the hall and walking in the kitchen. Nodding and following Carter's instructions Kisha walked down his hallway and into his bathroom. She closed the door and did some inspecting of her own.

Nosey as they come, Kisha shuffled around his bathroom and searched for any sign that a female laid her head here; however, to her surprise not one bobby pin or hair tie showed up during her inspection. Ladies, you know when a woman marks her territory the first thing she does is leave a bobby pin or hair tie, something small and petty however large and loud enough for other females to get the point; the point being "*Sis, he's not single so scram.*"

The absolute only reason Kisha started to search for any remnants of a female was because she was simply tired of dealing with in her words "ain't shit ass men" so before she got comfortable with any man she vowed to lookout for herself first and look for any signs of mess and or drama. Although she was coming up empty handed, she continued to search Carter's bathroom invading each and every form of his privacy. Opening his medicine cabinet, she noticed nothing much but a bottle of Tylenol and a bottle of Advil.

"Is everything okay in there?" Carters voice carried throughout his home. Catching her off guard, Kisha jumped up quickly hitting the door of the medicine cabinet causing a loud thud.

"Shit!" She cursed herself while closing the medicine cabinet all the way and turning on the faucet.

"Yes, everything is okay." Kisha screamed trying to disguise what she was really in the bathroom doing.

"Phew." She said while shaking her head, turning off the water and walking back towards Carter.

To her surprise in those short minutes she was gone he managed to set the table romantically. A few candles were lit, the lights were dim, while the smooth sounds of R&B played setting the mood. Carter was determined to break out the best for Kisha simply because he felt she deserved it.

It didn't take a rocket scientist to decipher that Kisha had her share of hurt. Carter had an innate ability to sense what people have gone through and he could tell that Kisha has been through somethings and judging from Kisha's mannerisms he could tell that Kisha was going to guard her heart like a warrior which slightly worried him because he knew that even if she didn't mean to, Kisha would make him pay for her ex's wrong doings. Even though Carter was taking a risk he was more than willing to do so because he saw something different in her. Kisha was rare and he sensed that instantly meeting her. Her aura and her energy was something he gravitated towards, her beauty was just an add on for him, it was a plus for him. Ignoring his thoughts Carter turned his attention back to Kisha and the curly fro' she wore that bounced effortlessly with the switch of her hips. During this dinner he wanted to know more about Kisha and not the guarded Kisha, or the Kisha with the somewhat hard exterior he wanted to be introduced to the Kisha that no other man ever got the pleasure of seeing and he was determined to get to that Kisha now.

***

"So, you mean to tell me all I had to do was cook for you and then you'd fall into my arms?" Carter asked Melanie with heavy eyelids while holding her tightly.

"Yep cook for me forever, keep your conversation interesting just like tonight and we'll end up like this every time." Melanie said referring to the two being cuddled up on Carter's couch watching the sunset. After dinner and conversation Carter asked Kisha if she could stay for a while. Truth be told he was just yearning to have Kisha in his arms. With his wish being granted he couldn't help but to feel the most at peace. Kisha's head rested on Carter's chest while he ran his fingers up and down her arm.

"Is that a promise?" Carter asked with his eyes closed.

"A promise." Kisha said through a smile.

"You know what I sensed from you?" Carter asked.

"What's that?" Kisha questioned.

"That you needed to be held and dealt with delicately, I don't know why I just feel this thing deep down inside of me telling me to protect you."

"You'd be a first to feel that way." Kisha answered honestly. Kisha had her share of heartbreaks and instead of the men in her life protecting and uplifting her they did the total opposite. So, it was refreshing to hear a man other than her father say he'd protect her.

"You know what my father used to say to me about men who don't protect the precious gems they're presented with?" Carter said lowly.

"What's that?" Kisha asked.

"If they knew better they'd do better. The protection of a woman is instilled at home, that's supposed to be embedded in your brain as young man. Unfortunately, some men aren't equipped mentally to take care of something as precious as a woman, so they scratch the precious gem instead of protecting it." Carter paused slightly and pulled Kisha closer.

"The good thing about that gem being scratched is someone like me being there to buff out that scratch, shine that gem up and place it on display for the world to know it's mine." He said while bending down and kissing Kisha's forehead gently.

Closing her eyes tightly, Kisha did her best not to cry. To some women this may be minor, or to some it may be just talk but to her it was much more. Kisha could feel the authenticity radiate off Carter, the sincerity in his tone was what made her the most emotional. From that moment they shared on his couch she could gage exactly who Carter was. Carter wasn't like the normal men Kisha dealt with, he was a real man and from that point forward she knew she had to treat him as such. Falling deeper in his arms she allowed her mind to calm itself, she allowed herself the opportunity to be vulnerable something she so desperately wanted to do for as long as she could remember. Carter allowed her to experience that and it was only their first date.

Brunch

Sipping from their glasses of Bellini, Kara and Melanie sat at their favorite French restaurant waiting for Kisha. Now normally by now they would've been salvaging their orders of eggs with turkey bacon and crumpets and on their third round of bottomless Bellini's but Kisha was running late and they didn't want to start eating without her. Looking down at the gold Rolex on her wrist, Melanie couldn't help but to blow out an exasperated breath.

"I swear if Kisha isn't here in 5 minutes I'm going to go crazy." She said while looking over at Kara.

"Just be patient I'm sure she'll be here soon." Kara answered while looking down at her phone and then up at Melanie.

"She better be, I'm starving." Melanie continued to complain. However, unbeknownst to Melanie, Kara's attention had strayed, and Melanie's dramatic outburst fell on death ears. Kara was far too consumed with the array of messages she received from Detrick. Smitten and full of smiles she couldn't shake the fact that Detrick was turning out to be everything she thought he wouldn't be. He was a gentleman, understanding and persistent. He made it more than clear that he wanted Kara and he would go through great lengths to get her. Truth be told after their last encounter Detrick was hooked more than anything. He feigned to be in her presence and whenever the opportunity was presented he took full advantage. Although his schedule was hectic he made sure to make time for Kara. And it was more than evident that the two were growing closer and closer. Texting Detrick back quickly and placing her phone on the table she looked over at a visibly annoyed Melanie.

"What, why are you looking at me like that?" She questioned.

"Oh, I don't know maybe because I've been talking to you for at least five minutes straight and you've neglected to look up from your phone." She snapped.

"Girl your ass is "Hangry", let's just order." Kara said, knowing that sooner or later this Melanie would surface. The Melanie that got cranky whenever she wanted to eat but couldn't. Turning their attention back to the menu's in front of them, they prepared to open it but got distracted by the royal blue Maserati that pulled up in front of the restaurant. Since high school both Mel, and Kara had a minor obsession with luxury cars mainly because of their lavish upbringings so by nature that's something they inherited. Admiring the beautiful automobile, they couldn't help but to wonder who owned the gorgeous vehicle parked outside of the small restaurant.

"Girl, who is that?" Kara whispered to Melanie.

"How am I supposed to know." Melanie whispered back.

"Look, the door is opening." Kara whispered once again. With their undivided attention focused solely on the person getting out the car their wheels started to turn when they noticed the well-dressed man exiting. Dressed simply in a Daniel Patrick sweat suit, the girls couldn't help but to conclude that whomever this was had a *"little change"* in his pocket. Watching him jog around the car and over to the other side they anxiously waited to see who was going to step out on the passenger side. With their eyes dead set on this mystery man's actions their mouths slightly dropped agape when they saw Kisha delicately stepping out.

"Oh shit." Both women said while watching their best friend ease her way out of this mystery man's car. While the women's thoughts swirled on the inside of the restaurant, Carter and Kisha indulged in their own conversation on the outside.

Standing in front of Carter smiling from ear to ear was Kisha; who still couldn't believe the night she just had. No, there wasn't any sex involved in fact she didn't even share a kiss with Carter, he just held her while they talked. They shared a level of intimacy that was foreign to Kisha and for once she felt she was in the presence of a man who understood her.

—

55

"I'm sorry I kept you last night, if I knew you had a prior engagement I would've made it my business to take you home sooner." Carter said while looking at Kisha.

"Please don't apologize, last night was amazing. One of the best nights I've had in a long time." Kisha said honestly.

"I'm glad I could do that for you. I'm also glad I'm the one that put that smile on your face." Carter said while gently grabbing Kisha's chin. Giggling slightly Kisha couldn't help but to shake her head at Carter's smoothness.

"It's almost like I can't stop smiling, my cheeks are hurting." Kisha said causing the two of them to laugh.

"When you're with me you never have to worry about not smiling, trust. I'll make it my business to make sure that smile never fades. I promise to make it my fulltime job." Carter said genuinely. Biting her bottom lip slightly Kisha placed her hand on Carters chest and started to speak.

"I know the girls are going to kill me already for being late, so I should get going." Grabbing Kisha's hand Carter leaned in and placed a sweet kiss on her forehead.

"Bitch! Did you see how he kissed her forehead!" Kara screamed on the other side of the restaurants window causing Melanie to jump.

"Be sure to call me later, okay?" Carter said while looking at Kisha intently.

"Okay." Kisha said while her beautiful brown cheeks turned a rosy red. Slapping Melanie's arm, Kara couldn't believe what she was seeing. The tough cookie known as Kisha was beginning to soften and right before her eyes.

"Girl, relax! You made me bite my tongue." Melanie said while placing her hands over her mouth and looking over at Kara.

"You'll get over it. We need to know who this man is though." Kara spoke will fully dialed in to Kisha and Carters actions.

―
56

"Well, we can get it straight from the source because Kisha is walking over here right now." Turning their attention to the entrance of the restaurant they watched Kisha float in with a glow indescribable.

"Hi girls." Kisha said while plopping down in a spare chair at the table they shared.

"Hey boo." Kara said while leaning in to give Kisha a hug.

"Hey girl, um who's the young man that just dropped you off?" Melanie asked getting straight to the point.

"Melanie!" Kara yelled while slapping Melanie's arm.

"What, I want to know." Melanie exclaimed.

"Oh, you guys saw that?" Kisha said through a smile while placing her purse on the table and situating herself.

"Uh, yeah! Stevie wonder could've seen what we saw."

"Yes girl, y'all were pretty cozy."

"He's just a friend." Kisha claimed while smiling ear to ear.

"Listen my male friends don't kiss me on my forehead."

"Exactly, passionately at that." Melanie added on.

"He's just a friend trust me, now what are we eating?" Kisha said while briefly changing the subject and skimming through the menu.

"Girl you better spill the tea, stop holding out." Kara said while taking the menu out of Kisha's hand. Scrunching her face up and looking in the direction of her friends she couldn't hold in how special Carter was any longer.

"Y'all that man is perfect, do you hear me!" She squealed while smiling and sharing the details of last night's dinner with Carter.

"Wait so he cooked? Like went in the kitchen and created something edible?" Kara asked while taking a sip from her champagne glass.

s, and the food was bomb! But forget the food his conversation was way better." Kisha said while sitting u p

"Now hold up, don't say forget the food now you now I'm a foodie" Kara chimed in.

———

irl, please continue your story." Melanie said while waiting to hear more about the fine man that swept Kisha off her feet.

Well after dinner, we ended up snuggled together on his couch watching the sunset. And when I was in his arms y'all I swear I felt so protected. It was almost as if I belonged there, like I belonged with him. It was crazy." Kisha said while smiling brightly.

As Kisha went more and more in depth the women couldn't help but to think about the new men in their lives. Kara nor Melanie mentioned their new boos to each other or Kisha, but they figured what better time to introduce the new men they were dating then at that very moment.

"Well since we're talking about new men in our lives, I want to talk to you guys about Brenden." Melanie said while sitting up in her chair and smiling slightly.

"Big head Brenden from high school?" Kara questioned. Giggling slightly Kisha took a swig of her drink and shook her head.

"Sis, you haven't seen Brenden lately." Kisha said remembering the picture Melanie showed her the night of their first date.

"You have a picture girl, let me see." Kara asked, while watching Kisha dig into her purse for her phone.

"Hello, I'm in the middle of talking." Melanie said while rolling her eyes after being interrupted by the two.

"Sorry." Kisha and Kara said while rolling their eyes.

"Now like I was saying, Brenden and I have been dating for the last few weeks and honestly I think he may be the one y'all. He's thoughtful, understanding and honest. He makes time to come and see me and he can make me laugh and he respects my creative space. He just gets me." She said.

"All of this after a few weeks?" Kara uttered.

"I know it may seem odd, but it's almost as if our souls are aligned. We just connect on a higher level." Starry eyed and full of positivity the girls could recognize how wrapped up in love Melanie truly was.

———

"Well Sis I'm not mad at you, you deserve the right to experience all of this! Just stay cautious and guard your heart." Kara said while smiling at the happiness her friends displayed while talking about their new experiences.

"I will girl, trust me. Now before we dive into this food and continue to talk about this new-found bliss in our lives; who was that texting you?" Melanie asked while smirking.

"Huh?" Kara answered while turning the half empty glass in front of her up to her lips.

"Yeah don't huh me! Kisha, while I was indulging in my "hangry" moment this one over here couldn't hear me complain because she was too wrapped in her phone."

"Oh, is that right?" Kisha asked while turning her attention to Kara.

"I don't know what you're talking about girl, I was just checking email-"

"Emails my ass; the only emails I smile at are the ones I receive from my personal shopper." Melanie said while cutting Kara off. Smiling widely and gnawing at her bottom lip; Kara figured the best time to tell Melanie and Kisha about Detrick was now.

"Fine, you caught me. His name is Detrick." She said while smiling shyly.

"Okay Bish, elaborate." Kisha asked while sitting on the edge of her seat ready for Kara to spill all her tea.

"There isn't much too elaborate on." Kara said while swallowing the lump that began to form in her throat. She contemplated on letting the girls in on the most intimate aspects between her and Detrick; mainly because she wasn't sure how they'd react and partially because she still was getting comfortable with knowing she hooked up and kind of committed txo a man whom she barely knows. It was a weird way to think about things and she knew it but that was how she was dealing with it and that's how she planned on dealing with it.

"Come on girl, what does he do? How does he look? Does he have any baby mama's, you know the norm?" Melanie asked while sitting back in her seat.

"Well if I knew I was going to get the third degree I would've kept my mouth closed."

"Here we go; she's getting defensive." Melanie said while biting into a piece of toast.

"I am not." Kara said quickly.

"Uh, yes you are. You only get like that when you're either hiding something or if you felt like you gave the goods up too- Oh shit that's who blew your back out the other day!" Kisha yelled causing a few patrons to look on.

"Damn Kisha, yell it to the mountain top!" Kara said while shielding her face slightly.

"Sorry, you know how I feel when I finally piece things together. But am I right?"

"Yeah is she right?" Melanie added in. Pausing slightly Kara bit down on her teeth a habit when she got nervous and finally decided to spill the beans.

"She is right okay, yes she's right! I had a one-night stand with the man that now someway, somehow is my man, yes she's right!" Kara said dramatically.

"Now bitch I didn't ask all of that." Kisha said while placing a forkful of eggs in her mouth.

"Kar' are you okay?" Melanie asked sensing Kara's slight change of mood.

"Yes. I mean I think I'm okay." Kara said while sighing and sitting back.

"What is it? What's bothering you? Did I do too much?" Kisha asked.

" No, it isn't you, it's just- Y'all I'm confused, like I'm not sure if I made the right decision."

"Well walk us through it, maybe we can *unconfuse* you." Melanie said while chewing on her breakfast.

"Bitch "unconfuse" is not a damn word." Kisha muttered.

"It doesn't matter; now back to Kara are you good baby, what's the problem?" Melanie asked.

"Okay; so, D and I met- "

"D, how ironic." Kisha said while smirking slightly and slicing into her Canadian bacon.

"Kisha shut- up please." Melanie said while shaking her head.

"Yes, please! Now, like I was saying Detrick and I met three weeks back at this upscale bar in SoHo. We talked, had a few drinks and then a few hours later I'm sprawled out in his bed laying comfortably under him and his Egyptian silk sheets." She said while blowing out a breath.

"That sounds amazing, what has you confused. Was the sex bad?" Kisha asked.

"The sex is beyond amazing! And from what I see so far, he's amazing. He's attentive, he's fine and he's tall."

"That's your type; what's the issue?"

"The issue is I feel like what I did was wrong, like I had no business in his bed especially because I barely know him. I just feel so guilty." Kara so honestly.

"Kara, you have nothing to be ashamed of. Society does a number on shaming women for doing the same thing men do. So it's only rig-"

"Here we go." Kisha said while blowing out a breath knowing that in a few minutes Melanie would fill their ears with her honest feminism.

"Here we go nothing. The world we live in tells us as women we can't own or act on our sexuality, we must be pure and wholesome. It's a fucked-up way of viewing things it really is." Melanie continued to say passionately.

"Listen, *Kimberle' Crenshaw* all that sounds beautiful, but I'm going to give you the not so politically correct terminology. Your ass is grown and if you need some vitamin D get you some and do so with no regrets." Kisha said while twisting her lips to the side.

"You know the only reason I'm not taking offense to what you just said is strictly because you compared me to my idol Ms. Crenshaw." Melanie said while rolling her eyes and looking down at her nails.

"The best way to serve a cunning insult is to add in a slight compliment, I'm so brilliant." Kisha said satisfyingly while smiling.

"Can you two not start, I really need to figure out how to get rid of this guilty feeling." Kara said dramatically while sitting back in her seat.

"Kara, you have nothing to feel guilty about: you may feel like this now but that's only because you've never experienced someone or something like what you're experiencing now. Sometimes that uncomfortable feeling you feel is God and the universe telling you to take that risk." Melanie spoke passionately and from the heart.

"Alright now, I'm not about to take it that far." Kisha said while twisting her lips to the side causing Melanie to roll her eyes.

"I'm just simply saying do what makes you happy. If you continue to have this confused, guilty feeling than go with your gut. If it stops than that means you're comfortable enough around that person to tolerate them even when sex isn't involved." Kisha continued while finishing her glass of Bellini and quickly signaling for another.

Internalizing the advice, she received; Kara finally felt at ease with her decision. Admittingly even after agreeing to give Detrick an honest chance she still had a bit of apprehension but speaking to her girls put her mind at peace.

Finishing off their last round of Bellini's, eggs, turkey bacon and crumpets the Women continued to indulge in their conversations, laughing, joking and sharing more stories about the new men in their lives. These were the things that strengthened their bond, that built it up ford tough. Nothing was more beautiful than seeing the big genuine smiles on beautiful women and too bear witness to the women's friendship was truly amazing.

5 Months Later

Come See Me

Laying across her bed, Kara tried her hardest to distract herself from Detrick's absence. He had a few interviews out in LA and 2 meetings in Atlanta, which meant he was on the go leaving Kara to crave his presence. Taking into consideration they've been joined at the hip for three months this small break gave Kara the blues. Reaching for her phone she decided to FaceTime her man and give him a taste of what he's been missing.

"What's up beautiful." Detrick answered, on the second ring.

"Hey." Kara said while sitting up and finding the perfect angle. Showcasing her green lace bra, she prepared to apply some pressure. Truth be told Detrick awakened a sexual beast in Kara one that she never knew existed. Yes, there was a connection between the two, but their sexual chemistry surpassed an emotional connection and that was something Kara would later come to realize.

Turning her attention back towards her phone; Kara was prepared to do whatever she had too to get what she wanted from Detrick and in this case, that was wild phone play.

"You already know a nigga' missing home why you calling me dressed like that?" Detrick asked while smiling slightly.

"Dressed like what?" Kara asked acting completely oblivious.

"You know what." Detrick said while stepping onto an elevator.

"I really miss you **Daddy**, like in the worst way." Kara said sensually while running her tongue across her bottom lip, knowing that would send Detrick into a frenzy.

"Yo please stop playing with me. I'll fuck around and come home right now." He said with a smirk.

63

"I wish that was the case." Kara answered while gnawing on her bottom lip.

"Let me call you back when I get in my hotel room and I get situated; make sure she's wet for me." Detrick said while looking directly at his phone. Nodding her head, Kara ended the call, rose from her bed and went into her closet. Although she was already clothed in a cute lace short set she wanted to spice it up a bit more, so she went searching for some sexy lingerie in her walk-in closet. Passing by a few things she finally settled on a crotch less lime green satin one piece. Walking out of her closet and into her bathroom she grabbed some coconut oil out of her medicine cabinet and lathered her beautiful chocolate skin with it, giving her an infinite glow. After prepping for her call, she looked in her full body mirror, fluffed out her hair and rushed towards her bed so she could be positioned perfectly for Detrick. As soon as she found the perfect pose a loud knock on her door forced her out of it. Sucking her teeth and sliding into her slippers she grabbed her robe wrapped it around her body and walked towards the front of her condo.

"I'm coming, damn." She said while unlocking and twisting the door open.

"Is she wet for me?" Detrick asked while standing in front of Kara looking as fine as can be. Dressed in a simple sweat suit, *Off-White vapor max sneakers* and a *Banni Peru* bubble Detrick had Kara's emotions soaring sporadically.

"Baby!" She screamed while jumping into his arms and wrapping her thick thighs around him.

"I missed you." She said while showering him with sweet kisses that later turned sensual.

"Baby let me get in the door first." Detrick said while laughing slightly. With Kara's legs locked around him he held onto her waist for balance.

"You missed me this much?" He asked surprised by Kara's embrace.

"You don't even know." She said while placing two kisses on his lip.

"Did you miss me?" Kara asked while Detrick placed her on top of her granite counter top.

"So much." Detrick said while quickly taking off his coat and tossing it on her couch. Standing between Kara's legs he began to rub her hips all while placing his head in the crook of her neck.

"I see you changed for me." Detrick said while admiring the satin get-up Kara wore.

"You like it?" She asked while wrapping her arms around his neck.

"Like it? Ma-ma I love it." He said while holding onto her waist tightly.

"You know what I'd love more though?" He asked.

"What's that?" He asked.

"You without it on." He said while pulling her closer and kissing her neck aggressively.

"So, take it off me." She moaned. Hoisting Kara in the air, Detrick placed her across his shoulders and walked towards her bedroom, to show her how much her presence was missed.

***

Laying her head on Detrick's chest while his arms wrapped around her full frame; Kara couldn't help but to run her fingers up and down the tattoo on his chest; a habit she recently developed. With both their bodies bare under the sheets and heavy eyelids they took in the moment of silence that surrounded them.

"Babe, you sleep?" Detrick asked, breaking the moment of peace.

"No, I'm up." Kara answered with her eyes closed.

"You sure?" Detrick asked again.

"Yes baby, I'm sure." Kara said while positioning herself closer towards him.

"Just checking, you know how heavy you sleep after I tear it up." Detrick said causing them to laugh softly.

"Oh please." Kara said through a smile.

"Nah but seriously, I want to ask you something." Detrick said while dragging his fingertips up and down Kara's arm gently.

—

"So, ask me."

"Would you feel comfortable coming to my game tomorrow night?"

"Wait, huh?" Kara said while looking up at Detrick.

"I'm saying, I want you to come sit courtside and see me play." He said once again while clarifying his words. Pausing slightly Kara thought of what to say. Although their relationship was progressing she wondered if being under the spotlight was something she was ready for.

"If you aren't comfortable baby I understand, trust me." Detrick said sensing Kara's hesitation.

"No, it's just, you don't think that'll stirrup a little something."

"I'm not asking you to wear a Jersey with my number on it, I just want you to come. Besides, if it does stirrup anything what would be the harm in that? I wouldn't mind the world knowing you're mine, shit; as fine and educated as you are I want everyone to know." He said honestly causing Kara to smile widely.

"I'm just saying, I don't see too many men in the spotlight with women who are shaped liked me."

"What's that supposed to mean." Detrick asked.

"You know what I mean; thicker women."

"Listen it's plenty of nigga's in the league that deal with thicker females; it's never publicly admitted though, shit is sad but it's true. Me on the other hand I don't share who I'm with openly until I know the woman I'm dealing with is someone I can build with and I feel like I can build with you."

"Are you just talking just to talk?" Kara asked while smirking.

"Never that, I'm just being honest. I see a future with you; I'm not scared to admit it. Never met a woman that truly intrigued me the way you do. I respect everything you do, from the way you carry yourself to the way you grind. The fact that you have your own just adds on to my attraction to you. I know that with or without me your shit is aligned."

"Damn, I'm pretty amazing." Kara said causing both she and Detrick to laugh.

"Fucked up the entire mood." Detrick said while continuing to laugh.

"No but in all seriousness, I appreciate hearing you say that. So many men I've dealt with in the past took those qualities about me for granted, so it feels good to know that they don't go unnoticed."

"That's exactly why those niggas are in the past."

"Right where they're supposed to be. Shoot, I know I'm right where I'm supposed to be."

"And where's that?" Detrick asked.

"In your arms." Kara answered.

"Heard you. No can you answer my question? Am I going to see you courtside?"

"I'll be there baby, with bells on."

"Good, I'll have a reserved room for you at Barneys tomorrow morning."

"No baby I'm fine. Have you seen my closet? It's like Saks on steroids."

"I insist ma-ma, let me spoil you." Detrick said passionately.

"I feel like it'll be an argument if I say no, so I'll be at Barney's bright and early tomorrow."

"That's more like it, now let's get some sleep." Kissing her forehead sweetly Detrick closed his eyes and drifted off to sleep with Kara quickly falling asleep after. And even though they were sleeping, their eyes didn't need to be closed for them to feel like they were dreaming.

—

Courtside

"Mel can you pass me that Gucci box in my closet." Kara asked while her makeup artist sculpted her already beautiful natural contour. After work, shopping and the salon she made it back to her condo just in time for her to get ready for Detrick's game later as promised.

"Umm, which one?" Melanie asked while looking at all the designer boxes stacked in Kara's neatly organized closet.

"The box furthest to the bottom."

"Found it." Melanie answered while grabbing the box and walking out of the closet and into Kara's bedroom.

"Thanks boo." Kara said while taking the lid off the black *Sylvia Web Black Gucci Booties* in front of her.

"I know I should be mesmerized by the boots, but I'm still stuck on the fact that you cut your hair into a pixie." Melanie said still shocked at Kara's hair.

"I know. I really wanted something new especially since everything in my life is new. A new love, new business ventures, new cars and an overall new outlook on life. I just felt like it was time for something new." Kara said while running her hands along the back of the nape of her neck.

Kara was more than satisfied with her hairs outcome she just wondered what exactly Detrick would think. She hadn't seen him since he left her earlier and she was dodging his FaceTime calls purposely. She wanted to show up to his game looking more than snatched, in fact she wanted to look so good that if her picture was taken she wouldn't have to worry about being dragged all through social media, she wanted everything to be nice and air tight.

"Well, you look beautiful girl, I wish I had the courage to do it."

"Girl all that beautiful luscious natural hair? Please don't." Kara said admiring her friend's beautiful mane.

"Hair doesn't make a person, if I had a shaved head, a low-cut fade, waves or long hair straightened to my back that wouldn't make me less or more of a dope ass person."

"Preach." Mya, Kara's makeup artist said while applying a thin pair of lashes onto Kara's already long ones.

"True indeed sis, true indeed. Now can you help me figure out what shoes to wear tonight? I'm thinking of changing these for a sexier heel." Kara said while showcasing the low Gucci Bootie she contemplated on wearing.

"I think you should wear those but if you want to change them then change into a classic classier heel. How about your Kates?"

"Girl, hell no. I always look like I have stick up my butt when I walk in those."

"I'm can't deal with you." Melanie said while laughing.

"I wish Kisha could've made it, we would've walked in there and grabbed you something cute to wear with a quickness." Melanie said while sitting back on Kara's bed.

"I know but money calls. She's the new accountant for Loman and Kasich's Firm so she's been swamped with work, remember last night she was telling us, she didn't even have time to see Carter?"

"Well we can't be mad at our girl for securing her bag and saving up her coins."

"Exactly that's why I didn't get upset when she said she couldn't make it tonight."

"Well 2 out of three of the Amigos are here so tonight should be fun, even though I have not a clue about basketball." Melanie said while glancing down at her phone and then up at Kara.

"Shit girl, me either. I'm just as lost as you; I'm going to support my baby."

"You better brush up on your skills girl, you must know more about your man's professions."

"You're so right, grab my phone let me search up some highlights." Kara said jokingly.

"Stop, playing." Melanie said while laughing and walking back in Kara's closet.

"Yes boo, find me something fire to wear!"

"Got you girl." Melanie answered back while walking further into Kara's palace of clothes.

"Okay, look." Mya, said while stepping back from Kara's face and holding up a mirror.

"I look so bomb! Girl, you did that." Kara said while moving her head from side to side looking at the beautiful "beat" she just received.

"It wasn't hard, you're already gorgeous."

"Thank you." Kara said while smiling widely showcasing her pearly whites.

"No problem." Mya answered back while packing up her makeup.

Hearing her phone ring, Kara walked towards her nightstand and grabbed it off the charger. Swiping her finger across the screen, she answered quickly.

"Hi baby."

"What's up gorgeous, what you doing?" Detrick's deep voice echoed on the receiving end of the phone.

"Getting ready to go see number 33." Kara said while smiling sweetly and walking Mya out.

"That's what I like to hear. I just wanted to call and let you know that a car will be there to pick you up at 6."

"Okay baby, see you soon." Kara said while ending their call and locking her front door.

"Kara, I found the perfect outfit!" Melanie yelled.

"I'm coming, I'm coming." Kara answered back while shuffling her feet against the plush carpet in her apartment.

"Oh yes, that's the one!" Kara squealed excitedly.

Now, Kara was more than ready for her man to see her.

***

"Girl they have our thick asses on this little ass golf cart; they better slow down." Kara whispered to Melanie while they rode through the arena and towards their seats. They were a few minutes late so the usher they were given made it his business to get them to their seats as soon as possible.

"Tell me about it I'm gripping this pole for dear life." Melanie said.

"Shit it wouldn't be your first time." Kara said while laughing

"Girl shut-up." Melanie said while rolling her eyes and laughing.

"No but seriously; how are you and Brenden."

"We're really good; I'm supposed to be flying out to LA this Saturday to spend his birthday with him." Melanie said while smiling from ear to ear.

"Girl look at you smiling all hard. You must really like this man."

"Like? Girl I love his ass."

"Oop, well excuse me I stand corrected." Kara said while stepping off the small cart.

"He's just so special to me like I've never experienced love like this before." Melanie continued while following Kara towards their seats.

"It's a beautiful thing to witness. Although I haven't gotten the chance to see you two interact I know just by your actions he's a genuine guy." Kara said while stopping briefly.

"Thank you so much Sis, but why are we stopping?" Melanie asked while looking at Kara slightly confused.

"I'm a little nervous; how do I look?" Kara asked while running her hands along her fitted blue jeans. She began to contemplate if the jeans and fitted tee-shirt she wore was too much.

"Kara, you look gorge, relax."

"You sure? Do I look snatched?" Kara asked once more for reassurance.

"Kara." Melanie stopped and grabbed her friend by the shoulders.

"You look beautiful so please relax and stop being so nervous."

"Okay, okay. Let's go." Holding her **Chanel** clutch close to her; Kara couldn't help but to switch her full hips slightly while an usher led them to their seats. The closer and closer the ladies got to their seats the sooner they realized how close they were to the court. Sitting down in her seat Kara blew out a breath and looked over at Melanie.

"I told this man I didn't want to be courtside."

"Girl if you don't shut- your ungrateful ass up and enjoy these seats; we're amongst the upper echelon of NYC, just relax." Melanie said while fluffing out her coils.

"Bitch we're the upper echelon, these rich ass aristocrats better be happy they're sitting amongst us. The chocolate Anna Wintour & the female Warhol."

"Okurrrrr!" Melanie said while laughing and shaking her head.

"Ooh-look there's my baby." Kara said while smiling and locking eyes with Detrick.

"Damn." Detrick mouthed while looking Kara up and down. He was supposed to be focused on the game that was about to occur, but he was far too wrapped up in how good Kara looked. Truth be told his mouth was watering for her. Short hair was her thing and he just knew from that moment forward it would stick with him.

Walking onto the court; Detrick prepared himself for the game. Saying a small prayer, he walked further onto the perfectly waxed hardwood floor with his team while the announcer continued his introduction. While Detrick focused up, Kara couldn't help but to get slightly turned on while watching Detrick in his element. Gnawing at her bottom lip slightly she sat up and watched her man run up and down the court.

"That's where he gets all that stamina from, lord." Kara whispered poorly, causing Melanie to look over at her.

"You need to stop."

"I'm sorry he's just, augh." Kara said while staring at Detrick.

"You're in rare form tonight. I've never seen you like this; especially over a man."

"That's because Detrick isn't just any kind of man. He's one of the realist men I've ever allowed in my presence."

"Girl you're over there sounding like you're in love." Melanie said while smirking and sipping from her drink.

"Not yet, it's getting there though."

"Trust me sister, I see that gleam in your eyes. It's already there. But walk in it, love looks good on you." Melanie continued while crossing her legs. Twisting her lips to the side; Kara allowed Melanie's words to sink in. She tried her hardest to stay away from the word Love; at least for now. She felt it was too soon to say but it was more than evident that she was very much so in love with Detrick. He completely stole her heart in 5 short months and he introduced Kara to a peace she thought she already had. Kara wasn't sure if it was his consistency, his supportive gestures, his affection. Or the fact that he made more time for her than anything ever; whatever it was it drew Kara in. It riddled her inhibitions and she knew for a fact that going with her gut was the best decision she could ever make. Detrick's actions proved that point completely. Grabbing her phone from her purse she snapped a quick picture of Detrick's jersey and captioned it *"Number 31"* she ended it with a heart shaped emoji and closed out the app. 5 months of dating and the two were extremely under wraps; never posted each other on social they didn't even follow each other. They kept it extremely chill and lowkey but at that very moment Kara needed the world to know that number 31 had her heart; it was a must.

***

"Listen I know your shorty is here tonight, but the team needs your undivided. We need this win bro; we need your undivided. Focus." Detrick's teammate said while they stood side by side on the court.

73

"Worry about yourself; I got this trust me." Detrick said while brushing him off and running into his position. Placing his hand on his knee's Detrick geared up for this major power play. 3 minutes was on the clock and he had to make sure his next move was his best move. Dribbling the ball a few times he then tossed it to Moe another one of his teammates who passed it to another who then passed it back to him giving him full access to the hoop. Sending the ball straight in; Detrick stepped back excitedly while being embraced by his team. However, his mind quickly shifted and traveled to getting his hands-on Kara. Looking up and over at her he watched as she waved her hands in his direction.

"Give me a minute; okay." Detrick screamed over the chaos around them.

"Okay." Kara said while nodding her head.

"Ladies please come with me." The usher who led Kara and Melanie to their seats said.

"No more golf carts, right?" Melanie asked causing the Usher and Kara to laugh.

"No ma'am, no more golf carts." The usher said through a laugh.

After walking down, a steep ramp; the ladies were finally settled in what looked like a green room.

"Thank you so much." Kara said to the Usher who kindly lead them to their seats and the green room.

"Girl these must be for you." Melanie said while pointing to a vase full of flowers.

"Oh my god!" Kara beamed while looking at the huge bouquet in front of her. Reaching for the white card that hung outside of the vase she read the note enclosed inside.

"I appreciate you beautiful; thank you so much for your support."

"He's the best." Kara said lowly while leaning in and smelling the array of roses.

"Girl this man made sure to give you all types of all star treatment I need to meet him." Melanie said while sitting on a couch that sat in the corner.

"I can't wait for you two to meet." Kara said while plopping down on the same couch Melanie was seated on.

Deep into their conversations the girls couldn't hear Detrick on the other side trying to get in.

"Wait shh, I think someone is knocking." Kara said while waving her hand.

"Who is it?" She asked.

"It's me baby." Detrick's deep sultry voice echoed from the other side of the door.

"Coming." Kara said while standing up from the couch and walking over towards the door.

"Hi beautiful." Detrick said while pulling Kara towards him by her waist not bothering to walk inside. Kissing her on her forehead once and then her lips second Detrick couldn't help but to fondle Kara's voluptuous frame.

"You look good. I like your hair like this."

"Really, I was afraid you wouldn't like it."

"You crazy? I love it. It shocked the hell out of me especially when I first spotted you. Had me all distracted and shit." Detrick said while licking his lips slightly.

"Distracted huh? Thank you, baby." Kara said while trying her hardest not to blush. Leaning forward Detrick began to whisper in her ear.

"What's the move for tonight?" He asked.

"Whatever you want it to be."

"I'm trying to pin your legs behind-"

"Ahem." Melanie interrupted; causing both Kara and Detrick to look in her direction.

"Come in and meet my sister Melanie." Kara said slightly embarrassed at how wrapped up they were in each other.

"Hey nice to meet you." Detrick said while giving Melanie a quick side hug.

—

"Nice to meet you as well. I'm glad I'm finally getting the opportunity to meet the man my sister's been talking about."

"I hope you've been hearing good things." Detrick said while looking over at Kara.

"Of course; of course." Melanie said while standing up from the couch she was seated on. "Kara my love I have to get going Brenden texted me a few seconds ago telling me he bumped my flight to tomorrow morning."

"Wait, we were supposed to be going to dinner!" Kara whined while watching Melanie grab her purse.

"I know boo; I promise you when I get back dinner on me."

"Aw okay; how are you getting home?"

"I called a cab don't worry." Melanie said while walking towards the door.

"Ok just let me know that you got in safe." Kara said while standing in front of Detrick

"Will do. It was nice meeting you again Detrick you guys enjoy the rest your night."

"Nice meeting you as well." Detrick said while briefly looking over at Melanie and then back at Kara. Between Kara's new haircut and the way her jeans hugged her curves it was hard for Detrick to look away from her.

Closing the door behind her Melanie preceded to an exit and quickly called Kisha. Answering on the third ring Kisha answered with a whisper.

"Bitch!" Melanie yelled.

"What's up?" Kisha whispered.

"Our Sister is in love!" Melanie said while pressing her floor.

"What are you even talking about?" Kisha said continuing to whisper.

"Kara, I'm talking about Kara. Today I finally got to meet the guy she's been gleaming about and girl when I tell you those two were lusty I mean it. It was so crazy my ass had to dip, I felt like if I stayed in there any longer I'd be in the middle of a porno." Melanie said while climbing into her Cab and closing her door.

"Are we talking about the same Kara?" Kisha continued to whisper.

"Why is your ass whispering?" Melanie asked while looking down at her phone.

"I'm sneaking out of my office that's why. Now like I was saying are you sure we're talking about the same Kara."

"Yes, girl I'm positive. I have never seen her like this."

"It was like that?" Kisha asked

"Yes, girl it was like that."

"Dammit, I always miss the good shit." Kisha said while rolling her eyes.

"Well what do you think about him?" Kisha questioned.

"We didn't get to talk much, they were wrapped up in each other. But I can say he isn't hard on the eyes and he's most definitely going to spoil her. Truth be told we experienced all-star treatment the entire night. Especially Kara, he had flowers waiting for her in our private green room and everything."

"Well they must be into each-other heavy."

"I don't know if it's there yet, but I know it's definitely getting there."

"Well, we shall see. Let me get back to work, I'm trying to get everything done before the weekend."

"Okay boo, talk to you later." Ending the call Melanie turned her attention to the small pellets of rain that developed on the outside of her cab's window. Cracking a slight smile, she couldn't help but to feel happy for Kara. Although things were slightly awkward with the three of them being in a room for a millisecond Melanie knew that Kara was finally living her best life. She knew firsthand how guarded Kara was when it came to men and if she did get into a relationship it would always be with the wrong people. She always dated guys that appeared to have it all together when in all actuality they were far too infatuated with their careers to notice Kara; so, to see a man treat her sister the way Detrick treated Kara put Melanie's heart at ease. Her sister was finally happy.

—

"So, you came to my place of work looking this good and you expect me not to get distracted?" Detrick asked sensually while walking around Kara with his hands tucked behind his back. Now that they were all alone all they could think about was indulging in a quickie before their dinner reservations at Bao. Gnawing at her bottom lip gently Kara parted her lips to speak.

"I wasn't that much of a distraction, you won right?"

"Oh, you being smart now?" Detrick said while stopping directly behind Kara, pressing himself against her. Bending down, Detrick allowed his thick tongue to graze her neck, causing Kara to dip her head back in satisfaction.

"You can't speak baby?" Detrick asked while removing one hand from his back.

"Uh-uh." Kara said just above a whisper.

"So, say something ma-ma, talk to me." He said while wrapping one of his hands around Kara's neck gently.

"Forget those reservations, I need you now." Kara said while biting her bottom lip. Smirking widely Detrick knew exactly what was about to take place.

"Too bad we have to wait." He said while pulling back from Kara.

"Babe, what the hell!" Kara screamed while hitting Detrick's shoulder.

"Now you know how it feels to be teased, that's for earlier this morning when I asked for another round and you did that hopping on and off me shit."

"That's not fair." Kara whined while grabbing her purse.

"That's not fair, let's go." Detrick said while mocking Kara and grabbing her flowers.

"You have everything?" He asked an annoyed Kara.

"Uh-huh." She said while rolling her eyes and walking towards the door.

"You mad now?" He asked while laughing. Ignoring him Kara continued to walk out of the door and towards the ramp leading to the basketball players exit.

"Yo, come here." Detrick said while closing the green rooms door behind him.

"No, you made me mad." Kara said while switching in her heels.

"I'll make it up to you later, I promise." He said while sneaking up behind her and kissing her cheek sweetly. Just that quick her mood changed, and her annoyance was replaced with a smile something only Detrick could do.

There was no denying that Detrick and Kara were on the road to something serious, only time could tell if this they got on was perfectly paved.

Can I trust you?

"Happy Birthday to my future baby zaddy, happy birthday to you!" Melanie sung while holding Brenden's cake.

"Yo, something is wrong with you." Brenden said while laughing and blowing out his candles.

"Baby you didn't even make a wish." Melanie said while putting the cake down and sitting on Brenden's lap.

"Everything I could've possibly wished for I already have."

"And what's that?" Melanie asked while smiling.

"A bag and my baby." Brenden said while kissing Melanie's hand.

"What a perfect combo."

"The perfect combo." Brenden said while kissing the top of Melanie's breast softly.

"No nasty time yet, let's open your gifts first." Melanie said excitedly while hoping off of Brenden's legs.

"Baby I told you I didn't need anything." Brenden said while shaking his head.

"I know what you said but I wanted to spoil you, you deserve it baby." Melanie said while walking towards Brenden's bedroom in his LA condo. The night before she managed to hide all three of his gifts in the closet in Brenden's bathroom. Grabbing the small boxes first Melanie rushed back to Brenden.

"Close your eyes babe." She said while clutching the boxes close to her.

"Alright." Brenden answered.

"Babe I'm serious close them. No peeking."

"Alright, alright they're closed."

"You sure?"

"If you don't come on." Brenden yelled.

"Okay; open them." Melanie said while standing in front of Brenden handing him the two boxes. Smiling and taking the boxes from Melanie's hand Brenden shook the boxes gently. Finally unwrapping the first box he stopped momentarily and started to smile.

"I'm about to beat you up." He said while pausing and shaking his head.

"Baby open the box." Melanie said while smiling at Brenden's actions.

"Oh shit!" Brenden said completely surprised at the diamond chain in front of him.

"And my daddy always taught me that you can't gift someone just one piece of jewelry you should always give them a set; so here." Melanie said while handing Brenden his second gift. Smiling Brenden couldn't believe Melanie's actions. He really didn't need anything and whatever he did need he was already able to supply it for himself. Being treated this way was something he wasn't used too. give unconditionally was something he had to adjust too. She gave him all of the things he searched for and that was balance, love and understanding. The gift giving was something he didn't need but was blessed he had a woman who was in a spot financially to give.

"A Rolex? Now you're overdoing it mama. Come over here." Brenden said while placing the Rolex box on the dining table. Walking over towards him Melanie fell into his arms while he kissed her face.

"Baby that's not it. You have one more gift." Melanie said while grinning.

"Is it you?" Brenden asked while licking his lips.

"You're so silly; that's later tonight." She said while walking back towards Brenden's bedroom.

"So, this gift is the one that's most special. It was hard for me to find but I knew I had to get it for you." Melanie said while grabbing the gift, walking out of the room and back in front of Brenden.

"Now babe be careful with this." Melanie said while handing the perfectly wrapped picture frame to Brenden.

"Ok." He said while peeling back the paper surrounding it; piece by piece.

"Nah what?" He said while stopping and running his hands over his face.

"Yo, how did you do this like I can't believe- oh my god Yo! Come here!" Brenden screamed while noticing the painting Melanie purchased.

"A Basquiat; how did you get this?" Brenden asked genuinely surprised. He was big on creativity that's what drew him to Melanie I mean that and the fact that she was thicker than a snicker. However, at this moment he couldn't wrap his mind around the fact that Melanie went all out the way she did.

"Well my friend who's well connected in the art world knew a few artists who were friends of his who purchased original sketches from Basquiat in the 80's. I was connected with one of them and before purchasing it my friend who specializes in art forgery checked it out. As soon as I received the okay I cut the check and this baby was on the first flight to New York. You don't know how many times you walked past it in my condo." Melanie said through a smile.

"Come over here." Brenden said while grabbing Melanie's waist.

"You're so perfect to me, do you know that?"

"That's all you."

"I'm serious Mel, you don't know how much you've changed me for the better. When we first reconnected, my mind was scattered I wasn't myself and this industry shit was pulling me into a black hole and then you came out of nowhere and completely changed that. You introduced me to peace baby, from the weird sage shit you put me onto all the way down to how you helped me strengthen my faith, babe all of those things made my life peaceful. I thank God every day for placing me in the presence of a Queen." Resting his head on her stomach he kissed it sweetly.

"I'm in fucking love with you. I love you Mel."

There was a brief silence and it was almost as if the words that escaped Brenden's lips shocked him just as much as they shocked Melanie. Grabbing Brenden's chin, she lifted his head for him to look in her direction.

"Do you mean that?"

"From the bottom of my heart." Brenden answered sincerely. Feeling the pace of her heartbeat quicken Melanie knew for a fact the moment they were sharing was extremely genuine. Parting her lips Melanie spoke straight from a place of love, there was no filtering or fixing she meant every word she was about to say.

"I've been in love with you since the moment you walked back in my life. You've treated me like a Queen. You took your time to get to know me, you just get me just like I get you. I love you just as much if not more." Bending down, Melanie kissed Brenden's forehead sweetly and basked in this very moment; the moment *of love.*

Meanwhile in the city that never sleeps, Carter was having his share of insomnia. In fact, for the last few weeks he hadn't had much sleep and Kisha was the cause of it. While his workload began to slow down, Kisha's started to speed up and their conflicting schedules were beginning to ware on his mental. Climbing out of bed and walking towards the front of his condo; Carter walked over towards his mini bar, grabbed a glass and the pint of *Hennessey* stationed next to the other glasses and poured him a drink. Turning the glass of brown liquor to his lips Carter didn't flinch one bit, in fact the smoothness of the alcohol settled him. Looking at the digital clock on his wall he wondered if it was too late to give Kisha a call.

"Let me just go to bed, my baby is probably tired." He said while sighing and standing from the stool he was seated in. Midway to his bedroom he could hear a slight knock at his door.

—

"What the fuck, it's 3 in the morning." He mumbled to himself while walking towards the door.

"Who is it?" He asked.

"Open the door and see." Kisha's voice echoed from the other side. Scrunching his face up in confusion; Carter began to wonder if the henny started to work on him just that fast.

"Kish?" Carter asked.

"Yes, baby it's me; now can you please open the door." Kisha asked while giggling sweetly. Quickly unchaining and unlocking the door Carter couldn't and didn't plan on hiding how much he missed her.

"It's late baby, what are you doing here?" Carter asked while hugging her.

"I missed you so much, I couldn't even sleep."

"You either huh?" He asked while pulling back and holding onto her waist.

"Not one bit." Kisha asked while holding onto her small Louis Vuitton overnight bag.

"Well come in and let me take that." Carter said while standing to the side and grabbing her bag.

"Look inside." Kisha said through a smile while plopping down on Carter's sofa.

"Snacks and alcohol, you trying to Netflix and chill me?" Carter asked while returning Kisha's smile.

"Maybe." Kisha said while smirking. Shaking his head, Carter emptied the contents of Kisha's bag and then snuggled behind her on the couch.

"I've missed you." Kisha whispered while holding onto Carter's burly arms.

"I've missed you more, I haven't been able to get much rest since you've been gone." Carter said while pulling Kisha closer to him.

"You either? I feel like a walking zombie It's almost like I have to be cuddled in your arms and if I'm not sleep just doesn't come easy."

"I'm here now just lay on me and relax." He said while stroking her hair.

"Carter, I, um; never mind."

"Now you know I don't like that, tell me what's up." Carter mumbled with his eyes closed.

"I'm going to be honest, since you've come into my life it's almost as if everything is just falling into place. You treat me like a queen, you listen to my spirit and you've learned how to talk to my soul. You've humbled my heart and opened me up to love again and all those things scare me terribly, it scares the absolute shit out of me. I've been heartbroken so much that after my last relationship I vowed to be done with love but then you came and completely changed my mental. I just, I don't know I'm scared, I'm just scared." Kisha said while allowing the salty drops of tears to fall from her eyes.

Vulnerability was Kisha's biggest fear. She didn't let men in, fearing disappointment would riddle her heart once again. However, it was different with Carter. He let himself in with ease making it hard for Kisha to dodge his sincerity. For once in a long time Kisha was open and falling in love.

"Stop crying beautiful, stop crying." Carter said while swiping Kisha's tears away with the pads of his thumb.

"Look at me, sit up and look at me." said Carter. With clouded eyes and a runny nose, she sat up and faced the man who held her heart.

"I am completely and utterly grateful that you've allowed me in your life, in your mind, your heart and your soul. I want to tell you how much I appreciate the way you check up on me throughout the day, how you come over after a long day of work just to rub my back and listen to me. Baby, you've taught me patience and how waiting for someone to open up is worth it especially when you care for them, you've changed my life. I know you're scared and I know you've been hurt in the past but I'm begging you don't make me pay for the others mistakes. Give us the opportunity hold each other hearts closely, give us that."

"Can I trust you Carter? All I want is to be able to trust you." Reaching over, Carter grabbed Kisha's hands and held them close to him.

"I can tell you to trust me all day and night, but I can't force you too. You have to know in your heart that I'd never betray you and once you realize that you've answered your own question." Falling back into Carter's arms Kisha allowed his words to sink. It was time for her to listen to her heart; it was time for Kisha to *trust.*

This is our life Now

"Baby, did you see this!?" Kara screamed while walking into Detrick's kitchen. Standing shirtless over the stove Detrick already knew what Kara was referencing. His PR team called him earlier that morning to discuss the stories a few blogs were going to break, they prepped him on how to deal with it.

"See what?" He asked while flipping a few pieces of bacon.

"We're all over the blogs. Look at this, who's the mystery woman pro-ball player Detrick B. couldn't keep his eyes off at last night's game?" She read aloud.

"Baby this is too much, how'd they get pictures of us leaving Bao's I didn't even see any cameras." Kara continued.

Not once taking his eyes off the breakfast he was cooking, Detrick shrugged it off.

"Hello babe, don't you hear me?" Kara asked while leaning on the granite countertop across from him.

"Yes, I hear you and yes I saw the pictures don't worry about it." He said nonchalantly while turning off the stove and turning to face her.

"Babe what do you mean don't worry?"

"Things like this happen all the time, especially because I'm in the public I've gotten used to it."

"Exactly you have, I haven't. I'm going into this blindly, I don't know what to expect. You know how evasive paparazzi can be, this is just too much-"Leaning forward Detrick grabbed both sides of Kara's face and kissed her sweetly.

"Baby you're overthinking this. Just relax you can't react this way every time we end up on a blog."

"Every time? Oh hell no." Kara said causing Detrick to laugh.

"Baby I'm in the public eye which means whomever I'm with will be there with me. That's just how it is, this is our life now."

"I know I just wasn't expecting it to happen so soon, it's just caught me off guard."

"Trust me I know, but the best thing for us to do is to continue to focus on enjoying each other. Let's just block out everyone else and focus on us, okay?"

"Okay." Kara said while sticking out her bottom lip. Standing there for a few seconds Detrick stared at Kara and admired her morning beauty; she was truly remarkable.

"Why are you staring at me."

"You look good as hell in the morning, especially in my t-shirt." He said with a smirk while pulling at his white Givenchy t-shirt that Kara wore.

"Thank you, baby." She said while reaching up and kissing his lips. Pulling away from each other Detrick spoke once more.

"Remember what I told you, don't worry about that other shit. Focus on us."

"I got it babe, I got it." Kara answered while kissing him once more.

Kara had to face the fact that being with Detrick meant change whether she was read for it or not, she had to come to the realization that this was her life now, this was their *life now.*

To be continued...

CPSIA information can be obtained
at www.ICGtesting.com
Printed in the USA
LVOW13s0324170518
577422LV00022B/287/P